INSTRUCTOR

A NOVEL

BETH FOLLETT

BREAKWATER
P.O. Box 2188, St. John's, NL, Canada, A1C 6E6
WWW.BREAKWATERBOOKS.COM

COPYRIGHT © 2021 Beth Follett
COVER ART: *Boy Heart Brain*, monotype, encaustic on cradled panel,
10 x 8 inches, by Anita Singh. Used by permission of the artist.

ISBN 978-1-55081-866-6

A CIP catalogue record for this book is available from Library
and Archives Canada

We acknowledge the support of the Canada Council for the Arts.
We acknowledge the financial support of the Government of Canada
through the Department of Heritage and the Government of
Newfoundland and Labrador through the Department of Tourism,
Culture, Arts and Recreation for our publishing activities.

PRINTED AND BOUND IN CANADA.

 Canada Council Conseil des arts
for the Arts du Canada   Canadä Newfoundland Labrador

Breakwater Books is committed to choosing papers and materials
for our books that help to protect our environment. To this end, this
book is printed on recycled paper that is certified by the Forest
Stewardship Council®.

for Troy, Ante & Felicia

&

Stan, with love

I wish once in a while to exercise my prerogative not always to act, but to explore; to hear vague, ancestral sounds of boughs creaking, of mammoths; to indulge impossible desires to embrace the whole world with the arms of understanding — impossible to those who act.

- Virginia Woolf, *The Waves*

forcing nothing, be unforced
accept no giant miracles of growth
by counterfeit light

- Adrienne Rich, "The Spirit of Place"

INSTRUCTOR

ONE || 1988

ONE

THE DAY OPENS in birdsong. A hermit thrush, sky above, lake below, concealed within concentrated shadow against pink light. Dawn chorus. Are you there? Are you there?

Somewhere a light goes out.

In the hour between wolf and dog — when a line of black thread held up to the horizon will distinguish itself to the human eye — Ydessa Bloom's husband, an experienced pilot, away in the north country on a fishing trip, plummets into a lake called Baptiste. The search and rescue captain, a lake resident, takes it upon himself to drive alone to Toronto. There, standing uninvited in her vestibule alongside the police officer charged with unpleasant duty, he explains in what manner Ydessa's husband and his friends died. Is there someone you could call to be with you? the men ask, and Yes, she says, there is, but No, never. She closes the door without another word.

Her mother, Rose — how she wails and shouts and tears her clothes when bad news arrives, when any new horror falls. How Rose and her father, Sam, will wail, forced to do the one thing they cannot easily or with pleasure do — wait. In their Swiss German tongue there is a phrase for a wordless thought that arrives in one's mind, a sudden flare, an impulse not yet formed. One would say of this flare: *There is a bird in it.* The bird comes to her: Go. She moves quickly, involuntarily. She assembles things one needs for a brief stay at a summer lake: cottons, linens, black lingerie, a sweater, folds these into a black leather suitcase. On the drive north, thought does not exist. When a thought presses in, she refuses it, though how she does so she cannot say. The atmosphere in the car is the pressure of resistance in June sun.

You scan your body from head to toe, looking for sensation, little pinches or twinges or aches. A dull, deep ache in your right shoulder, under the rotator cuff. Another in your groin. A third, yes, there, quiet but definite in the patella. To scan is your practice, a devoted daily observation. The day opens in birdsong.

The years of your youth, years when you grappled with

questions relational in nature — we who live next to this beautiful and venerable body of water, what is against us, what *for* (or against) the lake? — those years are gone.

So much in youth goes unthought, so much goes unsaid — so much longing can break the mind in two.

Some mornings you weep for your unlived life.

Your dedication to the lake, to lakeside stillness and contemplation, to listening, your disinclination to adopt the traditions and tastes of others, your interest in inner life, have earned you rude names over the years, though name-calling matters very little now.

You know how odd you are.

You observe the lake as morning comes, its language of balance, connection, of weights and measures, feeling its way toward shore, listening to itself as it goes, making inquiry, sending waves into subtler levels of its basin, images deposited on the basin floor, from which will rise a sphere of forms to hold you throughout this day.

Roger Campsall was an astonishingly handsome man. Ydessa thought life with him was made resplendent by his physical beauty, a life that rolled roundly beneath her sensitive fingertips. His steady voice — the surprising goad of it —

His body lies at a funeral home three hours north of Toronto. In the car bound for the north, where thought does not exist, where there could be no thought of hip bones, or of skin gone moist, supple, arousal in and beneath her hands, eyes opened and closed while small bubbles of harmonized sound escape slack lips, small sound rolling sinew, bodies naked and swollen in clean white sheets — between brief, slant light, no-thought streams north to the town of Bancroft. She drives fast, at reckless speed. *You're driving too fast, you're cutting too close. Stop honking.*

Roger, fastidious driver, safety-conscious pilot. One time, after one of her wild escapades, he asked for her wallet, removed her driver's license, tore it into pieces, set these alight in a glass bowl.

That will slow you down, my friend.

But it hasn't. No. Nothing has slowed.

The director ushers her to an anteroom and gently urges her toward Roger's body, its contours unfamiliar beneath a draped white sheet. She turns away, retching. After a while she recovers, then nods to the director, who lifts the sheet.

When Ydessa is sixteen years old, a beloved friend is lost in a head-on collision. One driver fell asleep at the wheel, his vehicle sped across the median into space already occupied, in a just-chanced turn of the head, words of comfort to the agitated Siberian husky whining in the back, now washed in blood, then again in a spray of lapis blue paint from blasted cans; the husky works her way out of the wreckage to stand obediently, unobserved, at the side of the road, blue tail beating dry earth. First responders arrive in emergency vehicles, step around and again around the wreck, begin work to remove the trapped body inside. For two hours the dog stands in cascading shadow. When at last the fire chief notices her, tries to coax her into his vehicle, she will not be moved.

Her friend's father asks Ydessa to adopt the dog.

I've never cared for an animal. I don't know how.

Good food and water, exercise.

She holds the father's gaze while the husky, now shorn of blue fur, naked, vulnerable, lies at their feet beating her tail against the step.

The strike to the throat — so much that can't be felt.

If the idea is to treat her like she's human, she says at last, I shouldn't be the one entrusted.

Whereas Ydessa was a cauldron, pitched in thought and intention, Roger was a steady wave, focused and relaxed. For their first date he had proposed a short flight in the Cessna. Arriving at the landing strip under a clear blue sky, the summer breeze soft and sweet, he'd said, We'll go up for a couple of hours. You'll have to shout over the noise of the engine. Do you want to wear plugs to protect your ears? I won't mind. Later I'll take you to a little French bistro — quite extraordinary to find so good a place around here.

Ydessa could have wept. She could be a cauldron and he would still take her to dinner.

She had watched the dashboard, fascinated by the dials, switches, and contacts, the red and green needles on the instruments oscillating in small, pleasant jerks. Roger held the controls peacefully. Takeoff into the dazzling blue was exhilarating, the shining expanse of farmland that rolled out below them widening, becoming woods, turning strange and piercing. When they banked to the north, it seemed as if some dead thing had come to life, raising itself inside her like a flag. Small lakes glittered like baubles, silver, flashing in the sun.

Sitting next to Roger with her hands empty of purpose, she grew anxious. Exchange was her occupation, moving people, things — a steady going forward. She was good at exchange, the golden girl of Toronto real estate brokerage, swift to move houses, connect people. To do nothing was to be overwhelmed by an unpleasant restlessness. Roger shouted above the drone of the engine. There's Stoney Lake. A turquoise-and-opal brilliance sailed beneath them. Commercial navigators use it to establish their bearings. It has a limestone basin, which accounts for that staggering colour. It can be seen from very high altitudes. Above thirty thousand feet, other lakes mostly disappear into the landscape.

His shouting was a dignified act, but to shout back would perhaps bind her to him. She studiously avoided feelings of obligation.

She had dated other men, had let a man's hard body fill her own. But always, soon and rarely too soon, rapture turned to boredom. If she could see through her lovers, if magic was effaced by an overactive executive function, affairs ended. Sometimes she simply drifted away, easily enough, so rarely did a man seek her out to ask where she had gone. She wasn't immune to convention — she understood the seductive appeal of a beautiful ring on a slim finger — but sometimes she questioned her loyalty to conventional romantic relationship. With time, misgivings gave way. She'd sell three hot properties in a row, be celebrated at the office by those who could afford to admire her without subterfuge, and questions of basic existence could be forgotten.

She observed the magnificent colour of the lake and said nothing. How impossible, in any case, to describe the beauty of light on the earth, its patterns ceaselessly generated across lively airs. She remained silent, held her tongue. The sky was sheer blue volume. There wasn't a cloud anywhere. Their line of motion dissolved beneath them.

Alone in her room, that blue sky, the slow and magnificent meal shared in the bistro garden, her robust effort to move things along (she had bowed her head slightly following remarks he made about her love of speed), unfurled in reconsideration. Quietly, outside his house, they'd uttered to one another only two words: *Good night.* The curious prop of *Good night*, she thought, a woman speaking low on one side of a car door, a man on the other. One of the most gorgeous scenes imaginable: warm air on a summer night, starlight expanding as desire expands. The stars might have been lining up into new constellations for their two hearts alone. He had taken her face in his hands, her hands had remained on the wheel. Well. Good night. Good night. He went inside and she sped away, each to re-enter their familiar rooms, draw in the day's net, feel in their skin some heat abating, heat still continuous in the heart, though her mind did wrestle with pictures it soon would bury.

She shot through the door of the anteroom, down a hall, out the front door to the parking lot. She knew she mustn't scream. Must not. Where was Roger's forearm, his hand; where was his wedding band? Squeal of tires, image of a hand grabbing hold of the wheel, clenched, restored. Authority.

Roger could not be the figure lying beneath that cloth.

Roger, come apart on the lake bottom. She refused to take this in.

She drove erratically through the town until she spotted a liquor store. She settled on a bottle of Scotch, asked the cashier if he could recommend accommodations, and stood stiffly as he gave directions to the Sword Inn on the main road. There was less urgency now, wasn't there, now that a strong hand was materializing. She would drink until nothing could harm her.

While the receptionist finalized the registration, Ydessa opened a brochure for an exhibition. Bancroft: Gem Capital of Canada. A picture showed tumbled apatite, quartz, nepheline, a treasure chest filled with smooth and polished stone.

Are you a collector?

A collector? No. She bent her head to sign the charge slip. Listen, do you know of any cottages for rent on Baptiste Lake?

My friend Barri sometimes rents her little cottage on Baptiste in June. Nothing fancy.

I need a clean place, very private.

Barri's cottage is what you might call rustic. No dishwasher, no microwave, no phone, no TV, no hot tub. But nice. Clean. Yes, private. Not fancy. Right on the lake. Glorious waterfront.

Call her, will you, and ask if it's available? I need two weeks.

The room was overly bright and smelled of stale cigarette smoke. Ydessa opened a window and closed the drapes. If there were other guests, she didn't hear them, didn't think again of the possibility of others. In the darkened room she considered her black leather suitcase lying open on a chair, the useless fancy lingerie. Do not think about skin no one will touch: incontrovertible, this fact first gaining then losing strength, an incoming, outgoing wave, vexation of a new order, perversity. Was it blind chance that had brought her to a dank room in a dingy northern motel on a June night?

A horror, she thought. Do not wail. Do not fall apart.

She sat at the desk with the bottle and a glass, drinking steadily as night came down.

Was someone on the bed, watching her as she drank, the Scotch like honey in her parched throat, tears rolling? Stop crying. Drink. She would not remember. She held the Scotch in her mouth, tipped her head, allowed the liquor to burn the soft tissue at the back of her throat. The room ceased. The heat, stench of old cigarettes, the unaccountable terror, dissolved. Night took up its numbers.

She was counting, swimming across an empty accumulation of numbers. She arrived at fifty wondering had she started at one? Couldn't have. Perhaps twenty, her attention too short to reach all the way from one to fifty. When had thirty come and gone? Start again. Behind and below the counting, intermittent sounds assembled and reassembled. Hands clapping to music, voices droning in irretrievable time. *Ydessa*. Time so impossible, she thought, always on the run, slack, then interrupted: clock such a crude measurement.

Who's there? Is someone there?

Her counting was a genealogy, a thrust of forward thought that cracked and exploded whenever she touched even lightly on words that must be resisted, shards in her mind, she a billowing thing that would be torn on the sharp edges of words in her first rage against the raggedness of all that flies against the mind.

T W O

THE SUN ADVANCES, you rise to watch another day begin, its colour drenching and amplifying the things of the world, which increase in number as light blends and cascades across the lake. You sit by the window. Anchorwoman releases a prayer onto the floor of things.

For thirty years you have made a cup of strong coffee in that kitchen then seated yourself in this chair.

You went to art college in New York in your twenties, studied music and painting there, your New York experiences raggedy, memories flown. All save the day on which you met Cleo Barnes, a woman you were forced to forget, but never that day, no, that wonderful day. More or less easeful had been your return to this lake where you were born, never a doubt but to flee New York, back to the arms of Baptiste. You sit in your chair by the window and observe, your eyes open then closed. Existence depends on welcoming morning and the lake like this, receiving it deeply, beyond its surface colours, full of its codes, its history. Soon you will rise and prepare the little cottage next door for a guest named Ydessa Bloom.

———

At noon Ydessa steps from the motel room into light. She suspects she looks like her mother. Waves of nausea lash through her belly and rise to thicken her throat. Sometime in the night she had built a small fire in the bathroom sink, feeding it with bits of torn paper and clippings of hair. The soot and ash left a grey ring on the porcelain, which water and hand soap have been unable to remove. Lifting on small drafts, a bit of flaming paper burnt a hole in the pink bath mat. She has the mat stowed in her suitcase.

She lowers the convertible roof, gets in behind the wheel, readjusts the rear-view mirror, catching sight of her cropped hair, her own dark eyes. She stares at their vacancy, doesn't hear the receptionist approach, is startled by her face as she squats by the passenger door.

I called my friend. Her place is available, six hundred dollars for two weeks. Not many people rent in June, as the blackflies are bad, though the fireflies — the fireflies will astonish you. Her name is Barri Grew.

A bright butterfly has landed on her left shoulder and is resting tenderly there, its small yellow body and its palmate wings lit by the sun. Ydessa stares. The brilliant light streams across the creature's wings, which gently lift and settle, open and settle. The hot leather seat grips her bare legs. She can taste the dust that fills the air, twisting and dissipating over cars passing on the road above the motel.

The receptionist stands and the butterfly rises hesitantly, up then away. She reaches across the seat and taps Ydessa's forehead.

Hello? Go to Barri's cottage. Barri Grew. Take South Baptiste Lake Road to Fell Road. It's the small white cottage after the causeway. She's expecting you.

Go to a stranger's cottage? Whatever for? She cannot make this fit to logic of any kind.

The butterfly reappears, hovering in the warm air surrounding the car. The world is quiet, drowsing. A warbler chirps. A weariness descends, a sadness equal to the beauty of bright yellow wings pulsing in the warm air. Ydessa lowers her head to the steering wheel. A great sobbing breaks from her at last and can't be checked.

The receptionist moves away, turns, and stops, observing the butterfly as it rides the air currents traversing the parking lot. She takes a pack of cigarettes out of her back pocket, opens it, withdraws one slowly, and lights it. Stands there, smoking and watching: not a cloud in the sky. *Chet. Chet.* The voice of a song comes to her: *Don't interrupt the sorrow.* Hearing that voice, she airs out her own voice a little. *God goes up the chimney like childhood Santa Claus. Darn right.* The woman in the convertible clears her throat. She turns back toward the car. Ydessa is reaching across the seats, her tear-drenched face craning upward.

What's your name again? she asks.

Teresa.

Call your friend, Teresa. Tell her I'm coming over.

Teresa takes another drag from her cigarette, her open countenance full of light against a background of open sky.

Sure.

Unfurling to the west of the town of Bancroft, Baptiste Lake Road rolls and sags, obedient to the curve of the lakeshore, a road lined with thick stands of evergreen that break occasionally to reveal a glimpse of expansive, shimmering blue. Between the trees the water flashes azure. She catches brief glimpses of lakeside homes, a few seasonal cottages, set far back from the road, partially hidden by cedar. She grips the wheel, racing beyond her overnight self, travelling fast with the ragtop down, dust rising, her feet bare, legs tense, eyes swollen and aching behind dark glasses. A black dog speeds over a green lawn toward the car, barking violently, and within her chest she feels her heart's blood explode. Her thoughts are tangling, chaotic. She wants a drink. All of a sudden there is nowhere in the world to be. This road is nothing to care about, nothing but a snarling line. And just as words of self-loathing are forming out of the snarl, a young boy emerges at roadside and steps into the windshield frame containing road, trees, her severed interest, and a dim vision of Roger on their wedding day, leaning into a camera, his grin loopy, Ydessa in mid-length Alaïa gown, iridescent green-gold clinging to her body like something wet and heavy, her modern tiara a delicate crown of stars.

She swerves, hard. A wheel catches the verge, the car plows into the ditch, drags to a stop.

She is halfway out of the driver's seat, and yelling. For fuck's sake — slipping and sliding in her bare feet on the ditch's damp leaves until she collapses in grass above a culvert.

The boy steps toward her, no perceptible change to his pace. He stands over her, blocking the sun.

Sorry. Are you all right?

She could tear him to pieces. She could wring his neck. She is so full of raving she cannot speak. Mustn't look at the kid.

He sits down next to her. The air fills with a kind of electrical snapping.

Move away! she shouts.

What might she do? There beside her, he is the very source of chaos, smelly, filthy, low, speaking like someone half out of a dream. Like a sleepwalker.

Do I look all right? she hisses, perceiving for a second time a terrifying thing flying straight for her, driving up into her mind, a mind so foolishly trafficking in imperatives at that moment, she almost laughs. She holds her knees and rocks back and forth, singing, No. No, there in the ditch, shoeless and raving, not yet free of the horror, the moment not yet averted, then, yes, averted. No screaming din of shattering glass and metal. Not yet impaled.

Sleep is so dangerous. Booze is so dangerous. Try to stay alert to the presence of the savage and the barbaric.

He has the look of a child who cannot be astonished, as if he has seen and heard every manner of outrageous adult thing. He wakes a little from his dozing. His attitude is soft and receptive, soft especially around the mouth, but Ydessa does not notice. She lets go of her kneecaps and stretches her legs flat out in front of her. The muscles in her thighs tauten then slacken, making her brown knees dance. She becomes absorbed by the clench-and-release, the sensation of blades of grass pressing into the backs of legs and knees. The boy sees how the tendons in her legs pull.

A car roars past, stirring up dust. She turns to the boy. He is staring after the car as it disappears down the road. A swarm of insects balloons behind his head.

Am I very far from Fell Road? she asks.

The boy keeps looking down the road, past the spot into which he had mindlessly stepped.

No, not very far. I could show you. He scratches his head, not looking at her.

You could show me.

Yes. I could come with you in your car. I could walk home after I show you.

She flinches. You almost killed me, and now you want to sit in my car and give me directions? My almost-destroyer, be my little navigator?

The boy looks at her, observing everything about her. How her eyes rush behind outsized sunglasses, her glance falls askew on things then flicks away. How her mouth, somewhat swollen, has lips that curl. She has chewed the bottom one. He sees how thin she is. Where are her shoes? He feels her anger. A burnt quality to the air around them, an odour like burnt metal, the air he senses like fine sand on his bare arms and face.

A wind is rising, clouds are gathering. Time is shortened. He thinks he will have to be careful with her, extra careful. Well, he is an extremely careful and considerate boy. People have said so.

I could go with you. Or I could draw you a map, if you have paper. Do you have any paper?

He removes a fountain pen from the back pocket of his jeans, and holds it aloft.

A map?

She lies back on the grass, closes her eyes.

———

With the question of Roger's rightness riding inside every nerve, Ydessa had tried, during their flight to New York, in her double-mindedness, to relax, to welcome the particular textures of their togetherness in the spirit of observation only, and she was failing. She tried to grasp the nature of her failure, Roger dozing beside her, the cabin quiet as they sailed above the landscape at thirty-six thousand feet. She considered his gorgeous profile. Roger was not what is wanted, was he? But. Perhaps.

She did not like New York, with its strange superiority, its inflation on the one hand and its terrific inferiority complex on the other, making a person feel small one minute, gigantic the next. Roger was taking her to his mother's penthouse on the Upper East Side. The thing was to steer away from him a little, she thought, watching Sixth Avenue slide by, yellow taxis on either side of theirs, in procession, crawling. Her hurry quickened. She reminded herself that this shimmering city was not to be theirs, not ever. Roger had abandoned New York's complexity for Toronto. She would not be caged, would not be pinned down.

Maybe she could relax.

World, world: once they were inside the penthouse, a glass of very expensive Scotch was placed in her hand. What is it? Bunnahabhain. Never heard of it. Three perfect Macintosh apples shone in a crystal bowl, their soft pulp hidden under waxed surfaces. They were never the proffered food but accent only. Around the rooms twenty mirrors glittered, small fluctuations of a hungry minotaur that prowled deep within the penthouse atmosphere. A Byzantine, three-storey hideaway in hues of blood, steel, and dirt, its complicated form — halls and doorways, stair-wells and inner sanctums shaped obliquely, tipping away from every standard grid — tripled by glossy surfaces. Roger's mother had bought and redesigned the penthouse after the sudden departure of his father, gone without a look back. Vanished.

Like a compass I will be for you, Roger had said as they rose in the elevator to his mother's rooms. Use me like a world map.

She stands and the boy rises also. She's dizzy, her thoughts race. Brushes dry grass off her legs and skirt. Tilts back her head to shift her focus, and thoughts vanish. A sudden sharp pain in the centre of her chest.

Look, stop it. I don't need you to come with me. I most certainly don't need a map. I can find the place by myself. Just up ahead, you say?

The boy nods.

In one motion she is back in the car. The boy takes two steps down into the ditch and pauses. He returns his pen to his back pocket then shoves both hands deep into the front ones. Through the rear-view mirror she sees him with an unexpected feeling of tenderness.

She leans out to look right at him. Stay off the road.

He nods.

The ditch is shallow, so she's able to back the car out slowly. She eases into first gear, second. In the mirror she watches the boy recede. The sky is a sea of high scudding clouds, light pouring like milk through blue gaps — soft gold, soft blue, milky light in a layered sky. Dust rises as she accelerates, the sky shines overhead, she gathers all she has seen into a point. Her head aches. She speeds along the road to the small white cottage where she will face the terrible question of how the world has come to be so cold.

THE BOY'S DRAWINGS — bird flight, insect flip, trees that bloom, the shift of a wave, multitudinous symbols that congregate, fluctuate, sets of lines that flow into new association. Bee. Mother. Prince. Within this confluence of symbols, generous festival, his hand moves the pen in small commotion. He wonders if, by his observation of the commotion, his inky diagrams change somehow. He worries about change. He spends nights awake, fretting, as time drains, flees, fades, moves like illimitable quicksilver. He has what he believes are his instructions: make sense of things, but do not break what you don't understand.

When his mother appears she speaks in riddles. Time, she says, enters fields where they lie most dark — time, roused by the sting of longing. It enters earth through winding passages, harrowed by husks of dead bees; it plunders water's deepest swells, aroused by heat to descend staircases made of stone, their walls whitened bone, death that has burrowed within mounting sediment, small pearl of light, rib and skull, the feather tooth, glint of sapphire star, a coffin hinge. Dark offerings: rhythm and weight of descent, senses altered as time thrusts against gravity, as it drops from memory, descending, to leap — blind, alert — from perfumed impression to cascading wave, dropping down to the honey line.

Ydessa turns onto a short drive. The small white cottage is hidden slightly by a circle of red and jack pine, the lake flashing like hammered silver beyond the trees. A white-haired woman crosses the waterfront in a paddleboat: she smiles and waves. Ydessa looks on severely, doesn't raise her hand. Her thoughts mix and pour like sand in an overturned hourglass until one continuous strand predominates: negotiate the terms of rental, get back to the liquor store before it closes. What an idiot.

Somewhere on this lake the nose of Roger's plane struck the water, and his life, the lives of his friends, ended. She would find this place. She had no boating experience, was no swimmer. Perhaps a man with a boat? No. The very thought of help — people asking questions, offering opinions, or standing before her, apologetic for the inadequacy of their words: she could not abide such deficiencies. No helpers.

Another plan, a bird with wingtips lit by flushing light, begins to take shape. A half plan only, darkly perceived. She senses an idea forming but does not think Plan. She is agitated, unsettled. Sunlight on the water dazzles, almost blinds her. She can see how the lake is alive with light, the sand golden where the water shallows. She smiles momentarily and forgets herself. In the ease of forgetting, a feeling of sudden liberation rises within her. She is back to her ceaseless craving for drink, while a robin sings its clear, high carol above her head. A dog's bark shoots out over the lake.

She calls out. Hello?

———

Twigs and dry leaves snapping under your feet, you come along the worn path carrying two plastic jugs, water sloshing and chugging. She has arrived. You put the jugs down at her feet. Where are her shoes? Her feet are bare.

You gesture toward the house. There's a tap just outside my back door. Use that tap for your drinking water. Don't drink the water in the cottage. It's all right to brush your teeth with it. Give me your refillable bottles, your used papers. Shower's good. Some tenants keep the blinds closed: I can see your bedroom window from my windows. Bed's very good. Its frame was made in 1948, but I put a new box spring and mattress on it last year. Do you like a firm mattress, Ydessa? Do I have the correct pronunciation?

Yes.

You are wearing your lumber jacket. Your faded jeans are paint-splattered. A bug net covers your head and face. You are a sight.

Your name is strange, Ydessa says.

You laugh. All my life, people have mistaken me for a man. Your name is not standard either.

No. So I'm told.

Her anger is perhaps daunting. You smile briefly then turn away. Let me show you the cottage.

Enter through a small screened-in porch. There are quirks, you tell her, pointing — the tap water, the windows, neighbourhood residents who resent the summer people, the country store on the road beyond the lodge, which opens only when it moves the owner to do so, the dishes that belonged to your mother's mother, the heirloom bedroom dresser and chest. You climb ahead of her on a short wooden ladder to an attic with a small triangular window that overlooks the lake, giving the little room a tree house effect. A small wooden desk and chair have always been the attic's only furniture.

When I was a child I used to paint here, you tell her.

Do you paint now? Ydessa is torso and head only, legs still on the ladder.

Yes.

She responds by pursing her lips, seems about to ask another question, then disappears back down the ladder to the main floor.

After Ydessa retrieves the suitcase from her car, she stands at the windows observing the lake, the wide sky filling with clouds, these the colour of ash and bone. She watches the clouds for a while. The air in the cottage hangs heavy with the smells of ancient surroundings. She turns her attention to the path that leads down to the dock. She can name none of the wildflowers along the waterfront. Cedar, she knows. That is something. In childhood her mother gave her colouring books of the trees and birds of Canada, hoping Ydessa would learn these then point them out to her, but most often she found Ydessa lying on her bed, face pressed into the books, legs flung wide, arms limp, in an attitude of utter defeat. Get up! Rose would cry, appalled. We need your little light. Go outside, Ydessala, and study the birds by sight if you don't want to colour them.

She wants to go back to town. Get a bottle of Scotch. Get a book about wildflowers.

Jesus, she's forgotten Wilson. O sweet disaster. Will Barri allow a cat at the lake?

A great blue heron lifts from where it has been feeding at the water's edge. The sun is low in the sky, and as the heron rounds a point of land, its wings take the orange light, swift blessing. Ydessa watches from an armchair, drinking, while colour slides out of the sky and drains away.

She will have to drive back to the city to retrieve the cat. She must call Roger's mother. Could she go back to Toronto without letting her parents know she's been away? No, unwise to deceive them.

No phone in the cottage. She will have to disturb Barri.

She rouses herself, stumbles up the short path to the big house. Presses her face into the screen door, peering into the mudroom.

Barri is standing at the kitchen sink.

Sorry to be a pain in the ass. Is there a phone I can use?

No trouble. Barri comes toward her, smiling slightly, and Ydessa can see that, by anyone's standards, without the mosquito net to hide the fact, she is a remarkably handsome woman.

No answer in New York. She calls her parents.

Horrible, Ydessala, horrible. But why do you have to re-enact the tragedy? It is maudlin. I want you to get out of there.

No, Poppa.

She can hear him heaving himself into a chair.

You have to call Roger's mother again. You have to make a proper funeral. Don't make a mess, sweetheart. You have to come back. Get the grip.

Get *a* grip.

What?

It's get *a* grip.

Come back. You have to call the rabbi. The synagogue will take care of the details. You won't have to do anything. They will call the funeral director, they will transport —

— No.

Pish. You must be responsible. Get home now.

There is some shuffling.

Here, Rose wants to speak to you.

No.

She hangs up.

Barri's dog, a golden Lab, lies on the polished hardwood floor, thumping its thick tail, watching her.

You have the grip? she asks the dog. Fetch the grip. Good dog.

The sky aflame with fiery cumulus that ride over Baptiste, the top of an ancient oak crowned with ruby. You turn along the side of the darkling house till you come to the path that descends to the dock. You stop to look at the lake in its deepening hollow, its brilliance disappeared in evening shadow. The sounds of the lake open around you, wind in the rigging of a neighbour's catamaran, someone playing Patsy Cline, "I Fall to Pieces." Soft wind sighing through the pines. You think of yourself as a lucky woman. You stand in the coming night waiting for the night's fireflies to begin to swoop. You note that Ydessa has left all the cottage lights off.

Ydessa listens to the slow progress of a plane, in and out of clouds overhead. She can hear it groan as it surges above the wind she hears in the tall pines. A dog barks, followed by a man's scolding shout. She stands long at the windows, aware of her dim reflection, overcome, taking no measure of grief. Somewhere out there Roger's plane slammed into the lake in a tremendous downward plunge, thrusting the waters aside.

She will find that place of parted waters.

A week ago in sleep Roger thrust his arm out to catch a football, and sent his bedside table with coins, alarm clock, and small reading lamp flying. Everything hit the floor in a crash. Ydessa rose up out of an exasperating dream, shouting, Stop refusing me!

What is she doing at Baptiste Lake? Why has she come? She stretches out on the bed, her senses perilously disturbed. She has consumed only Scotch, her equilibrium is lost. Forgot the cat. She laughs bitterly. Sorry, Wilson.

Of Ydessa her parents had said, She will have her birds: ideas, magic, something to engage with, something to follow, some line leading her forward. Dreamy child. Curious child. Now follow is stymied, just hold on for dear life on a high ledge, as if blindfolded, as if bargaining, conspiring, with the devil. Just a little longer, says the devil. Everything will soon be over.

Her body, a great ocean liner, rolls through the night.

When daylight enters the room, it finds her sprawling. To jump wide of the day's demands, to deny the fiery anger pricking her heart, the fiendish self-pity chattering obsessively, is all she wishes to do, but she must rise, refuse the bottle, meet the day's obligations, and get beyond them. Get close to your life, she tells her rumpled reflection in the mirror above the sideboard, her hand around the neck of the bottle, imagining it shattered by the sheer force of her fury.

In four hours she is back in Toronto, back in the condo, talking on the telephone to the funeral director in Bancroft, to Alicia in New York, the two of them making strange, the talk of Roger's impossible death, their feet hovering above ground no longer solid.

She drinks throughout the day from a shot glass while speaking to the rabbi, then from a lowball glass while taking unwanted calls from Marc, her boss. How long will she be away from work? That's all he wants to know. She drives to her parents' place, and while their backs are turned steals swigs from a bottle on their happy hour cart.

Her tongue swells. Mean-spirited arguments unfold.

Sandwich, Ydessa?

No.

Eat a little something, darling. Would you like some cake maybe?

No. Nothing. *Nothing.* Or is it five o'clock? Let's have a drink.

Rose cries, There is a way to die, a way to bury a husband. You are humiliating the dead! Do you think you are just your own self in this house, with no one tied to you?

Ydessa agrees to pin a torn black ribbon to her dress, to sit shiva. Three days only, not seven. Her father says to his friends, For Ydessala, everything is negotiable. She benched gomel. This is wrong. She must forever refuse convention. It is who she is. One friend replied, Never mind. *Di tsayt iz der bester dokter.*

Roger's mother insists on cremation, the ashes to be sent to her in New York. It is forbidden! Sam whispers. Unable to travel (the sheer magnitude of her despair), Alicia sends a bouquet of white lilies; an enclosed note reads *I feel your pain.* Like hell — But there is no way to finish these thoughts. Jews do not send flowers. Jews do not isolate themselves at times like these. Rose turns from the lilies in disgust. With such money as Alicia Campsall possesses, such ease to reserve a private jet. . .

Ydessa phones to tell you she will officially begin her sojourn in six days. With a cat?

All right. Yes, fine. Do come back when you can. It will be good to have you with us.

FOUR

THEY HAD BOTH owned cars, but, finally, Ydessa was the driver. Roger loved expensive restaurants, Ydessa Sunday drives. They were heading to the Niagara wine region for a scheduled tour when she said, Let's go to Lion's Head, near Wiarton, instead. That garden. What's it called?

Larkwhistle? It's a two-day trip, to see it properly.

We'll get a hotel room.

Roger, usually so accommodating, this time had argued. She heckled him, said he was getting doughy, fusty. So he relented.

In the Larkwhistle garden, out of sight of the gay owners, Roger manoeuvred her up against the wall of a shed and pressed his body playfully to hers. Her submission surprised her. Keen desire overtook her. She dropped to her knees, receptive, uncaring in this rousing, uncontrived moment. In no time he was inside her, down in the muck, and they came together, mad, crying.

He is the perplexing beloved, their bodies completely unalike and his now shimmering. His has been lost and hers must be recovered.

Ahead of Sam and Rose, dazed and furious, she hurries along a narrow aisle past outstretched hands that brush her sleeves. She pushes toward the back of the synagogue, refusing all gestures of condolence.

Three hours pass — whose ends are the prayer service's beginnings, outstretched hands again brushing her cheeks — after which Sam and Rose take her out to dinner at their favourite terrace. They extol the courage she's shown, fret over her refusal to eat.

While she drinks her whisky, they attempt to dissuade her from returning to the lake. Her eyelids droop. To them she appears to be grimacing. Her expression is unreadable, uncontrollable. They fall silent, subject to fleeting, disturbing thoughts that must not be acknowledged.

It is the grief, Sam thinks. She is lost in the lake. He excuses himself. I must have air, and Rose cries, But we are at the outdoors!

He shushes her with a flip of his hand.

Ydessa inspects the items on the table: a squeezed lemon wedge, an untouched drumstick, a bouquet of peonies crawling with ants, an empty bowl. She is adrift in random thought, wondering if she could ever be happy in a rural existence, whether she could be faithful to it.

I'll never marry again.

Pish. Shush.

All is silence and finally no words to say it. Tired euphemisms drift as hands remove glass after empty glass, graceful, courteous hands bring warm honey, berries, water. *Drink Scotch. Study the sky and the clouds. Learn to swim. Learn to recognize wildflowers. Fucking trees.*

At another table someone is telling an old tale about virtue, how because a human heart, weighed at death to find what greed it held, weighed more than a feather, its bearer was sent to the underworld. She remembers a feather that lay beside the boy in the ditch on the Baptiste Lake road. She does not know the names of birds. Just bird. Bird, feather, flower.

When Sam returns to the table she stands. Take me home.

Henry Rattle is scuffling his feet on the dusty path at the back of the cottage. She won't come back, he says.

You look at the boy. He continues to pitch small stones he's gathered from the sandy shore.

Why say that? Your whole life has proved again and again that what you think is impossible is not always impossible.

He closes his eyes, expression fixed.

This time it is. This time it is impossible.

And why is that?

But Henry has pursed his lips and will say no more.

He stood next to his father, a beekeeper, watching over his shoulder as many bees gathered to settle on his open unprotected hands, a small mudra of bees. He wound them into a kind of comb, one hand wrapping strands of honey around their tiny bodies until they were encased in a honey cocoon. Their bodies startlingly yellow, bright, their buzzing muffled by the glistening encasement. It is a dream, he thinks, or else the bees would drown.

In the morning she gathers Wilson into his carrier and heads for the lake. The distance between old routines and as-yet-unknown new ones is what she says she needs, a distance to minimize what might otherwise defeat her. Two weeks away from family, from the pressures of Marc at the office, from the noise and relentless movement of the city and its restless citizens. Whenever she started out on a Sunday drive with Roger, he would say, This'll get the cobwebs out. That's all she needs, a two-week Sunday drive. Two weeks to become familiar with new routines — then she can move on. At the cottage she can ambush cobwebs in pursuit of the day that must come, when she'll be herself and sensible again.

Did she believe that distance from familiar things would assuage the brow-beating assailing her? That she would not capitulate to the disturbances in her body? That Roger, his soothing reassurances gone, would not gain fuller strength in death than he'd had in life? She had pursued her goals directly, without question, sure of success. In her early pursuit of Roger, she had stumbled briefly into boredom and ambiguity, but with the big diamond on her finger, she'd regained direction.

She would go to Baptiste Lake, be safe from prying eyes. Find the site of Roger's crash. Hire someone to dive. After two weeks, she'd return to work, composure regained, forward movement assured.

This was the thinking of the blasted widow who headed to Barri Grew's small cottage on Baptiste Lake.

IT WAS YDESSA Bloom's husband who flew that plane, the one that crashed, Teresa announces as she walks into your big house.

You stop stirring the soup. I know, you say. Henry was outside the cottage today, pitching his stones. He told me he had met the lady, meaning Ydessa. He was knocking about here for over four hours.

She's back from Toronto?

Yes. Came this morning but hasn't come out of the cottage. Henry didn't think she'd come back.

Teresa hangs her jacket on the back of the mudroom door. She takes cigarettes and lighter out of her jacket pocket. There's a funny smell in here.

You tell her you found a drowned rabbit this morning.

A drowned rabbit. That can't be good.

Nope.

Teresa lights a cigarette.

I found it rolling on the shore. As I carried the poor thing around to the back door, Henry sat up. He'd been grovelling, but when he saw me he got up, came over to investigate. He turned wild-eyed, cringed. The wet sandy body, its flattened fur. Couldn't say a thing. Then everything came together: dead rabbit, three men lost, strange woman at the lake. He clamped his hand over his eyes and started jabbering a mile a minute. Then he beat it out of here.

Teresa places her cigarette in an ashtray and goes to the cupboard to fetch wine glasses. A pleasant tinkling as she sets them down.

Why does a rabbit drown?

I don't know, you say. It's unusual. Rabbits can swim, though they despise water. Was it thrown into the lake? I think it may have been a victim of some lawlessness.

Teresa takes a bottle of white out of the refrigerator and pours each of you a glass. Your medicine, she says, and hands you the wine. She replaces the cork, returns the bottle to the fridge, and retreats to the mudroom for another pull on her cigarette. Sad, isn't it, how rabbits will wait too long. I've heard stories about them refusing to abandon fields set on fire. Maybe they have opposed instincts.

Rabbits are Fear Callers. It's said if you dream of a rabbit your freedom is threatened.

Teresa stubs out her cigarette and re-enters the kitchen. One thing I do know is, if Henry becomes more alarmed by what the rest of us simply fail to see, with no one to offer guidance now and again, he'll be an adolescent basket case. As for the widow Bloom —

— who will be my tenant over the next couple of weeks, you caution.

I haven't been thinking of direct intervention.

You take a sip of wine. Roger Campsall was a commercial pilot. The Cessna was his. He and his friends were registered at the lodge and had a fishing guide. Roger was originally from New York. A very handsome man. Cultured. Athletic. An experienced pilot.

Henry knew all this?

No. Even an expert pilot can get into trouble. A plane might have latent mechanical trouble. Fuel might suddenly cease to flow. But why did they take off before sunrise and without their guide? They still had two more days scheduled. I remember that morning. Absolutely star-studded and clear.

A hummingbird flashes at the window. You turn your head — gone, trailing a purr of wingbeat. Tangerine light streams through the lakeside windows. The radiant room. The cutlery, the glassware, glimmers. Your thinking opens and expands. Thinking rises between thought and gaps of no-thought. What is to be done? Are you under some obligation to help this stranger? Here she is, unexpected though not unwelcome, with her grief and her secrets, her bottles of Scotch, her hope to gain something at the site of her loss, her wish to kill suffering. And here is Henry, with his yearning, his strange proclivities, and Teresa, with her compass, her fixed beliefs, both of them already magnetized by Ydessa.

The table is set, the sun is departing in shades of blood orange, red, and magenta, dropping behind the trees, evening colours flowing over the darkling shore.

This woman, Ydessa Bloom, young and lovely, successful, in her shiny new convertible, her smart clothes, fashionable Toronto address printed on her cheque — so surprising, anything so new and shiny such a rarity at Baptiste. Henry is investigating her, he's already rapt. Where are her people? What sort of people allow a woman recently bereaved to leave the circle of their support and travel alone, anywhere, but especially to the site of the tragedy? It's common decency at least to accompany one so bereaved. But to stay behind and watch her go? Unless Ydessa has commanded it? Or has no one asked, What will you do at that lake? Perhaps no friend has heard of the crash, of her plans to come to Baptiste. No. Word always gets out.

She may stay as long as she likes. You will tell anyone who calls that the cottage is booked for the summer.

You turn. Teresa is standing at the table, glass empty, bottle raised in question. You nod yes.

Perhaps the emptiness she feels stretching out before her, no one to share the wretched emptiness, maybe it's a much older condition? Perhaps she had already wondered about going on alone?

Teresa fills your glass then disappears into the mudroom for another smoke. We'll find out more eventually, she calls, breaking your concentration.

She's not exactly the daughter of disclosure.

You can hear Teresa sigh deeply, dragging on her cigarette, exhaling. She mutters, I shouldn't drink. Drinking gives me ideas. She comes back into the kitchen. Or is it you? Does the scheming begin whenever I'm with you?

She sits down at her place at the table, takes hold of her spoon and fork, and begins to bang them softly on the tabletop.

We're not a *People* magazine article, is what you're saying. Let discretion be the better part of valour, you advise. Fine. So when do we eat? I'm starved.

You stood at the kitchen counter, your vintage glass bowls filled with green salad. You carried the bowls to the table.

You have a proposal, you said to Teresa.

Yoga. She was smiling broadly. My answer to just about anything.

The two of you ate in silence as twilight descended. Out on the silvering lake an approaching motorboat cut its engine. Small voices talking low. You who so often ate in silence, appreciated silence even in Teresa's company. So many sounds. A creeping sorrow rose in you as you remembered Henry, his face grim above the dead rabbit, one

more calamity at the end of a row of calamitous days. He had begged
you not to tell his father about Ydessa on the highway.

You stood impulsively and pushed away from the table.

Let's go down to the dock.

Shall I clear away the bowls?

No. Leave everything. Just bring the wine.

The moon was rising. A man and his boy were fishing. The
boy threw his line, calling out, I'll catch him this time, Papa, but
the man's reply, too faint, gave no emphasis one way or another.

Roger was born into a wealthy New York family and had already
inherited much of his father's wealth by the time he and Ydessa
met. He wanted to be transparent with her, said he had five million
invested, stood to inherit another ten million when his mother died.
He spent money in a measured, conservative way, and promised to
share all he had with her over a long marriage.

She was worth considerably less.

She envisioned trips, to Tuscany, South America, Sri Lanka,
Roger a fearless tour guide, she at the wheel of fast cars. He had
been part of an airline culture, dining out with colleagues, cheerful,
kind, unassuming, courteous, exchanging cities and beds night
after night. The gay men he worked with, with their model good
looks — androgynous, hairless Calvin Klein sylphs. Ydessa was
also androgynous and sylph-like. People commented on her lean,
inscrutable nature, so unlike that of Roger. She had wanted the
marriage to operate below the radar.

And now everyone will know.

———

Under twilight sky, a tableau, as you would describe it years later: two women friends drinking at a wooden table, stars burning above. The further each moved into the funnelling corkscrew of time and nightfall, the closer she got to the cliff of a star, searching for subtle and perfect harmonies. The slower each of us spun, the heavier the other got, until the pace of approaching night became imperceptible. Slow, slow. June night, heavy in fragrant descent, without wind, without cloud. Distant shoreline voices rose, settled. Peace came.

Inside the house, Teresa places a pot of water on the stove and in it a porcelain bowl of cut strawberries, to warm them over steaming water while she whips cream in a mixer. As the pot begins to heat and the kitchen begins to fill with steam, she stands at the stove, absentmindedly raising warmed strawberries to her lips, the bitter-sweet juice. The taste of so many Junes fills her. She cuts two pieces of shortcake, arranges the strawberries, adds the cream. She carries the plates to where Barri is stretched out on the sofa. In the kitchen again, she brews black tea. Her body, so serene on the dock beneath the stars, is now jumping with an angry pulse. The teacups rattle in their saucers as she carries them into the living room.

Henry's new mother, Teresa Rattle, she snorts.

Barri smiles.

Teresa sits, sipping the tea, observing Barri, allowing her restlessness to subside.

She begins to speak about the hearing stages of a yogi. Deaf to noises in the outside world, she will at first have a perception of violent wild sounds — ocean, thunder, waterfall. Then those with more musical structure will rise — bell, horn — and strengthen. Finally the hearing will become extremely refined, attuned to sounds of flute or bee.

I've never heard the waterfall. How far I have yet to go before I hear the bee!

A knock comes early to the door. The young boy, sleepwalker. He presses his nose to the screen. I saw your car.

In his striped T-shirt and dirty jeans, hair hanging heavy over one eye, the sight of this strange boy — a barnacle — makes Ydessa's throat dry up, her body thicken with feeling.

May I come in? he asks, after a while.

Ydessa holds the door open, allowing him to enter. Inside the cottage, he bends down and removes his sneakers. He wears no socks and his feet are filthy. He walks over to the windows and looks down to the dock just as Wilson pounces on an unsuspecting ant.

I like cats.

The sun rising over the lake, floating stars sink into grey-blue waters. A morning mist drains upward. The sun fights its way down. A chipmunk, searching for food at the edges of the dock, its body quick and darting, hurtles past Wilson, who has entered this strange new world in a poised calculus of stealth. Three yellow leaves drift slowly to the ground at his feet. A paw shoots out, traps one. Ydessa observes these small movements with mild interest, sitting on the dock, one hand holding closed a blanket draped around her shoulders like a shawl. The boy sits in grey underwear at the edge of the dock, swinging bare legs and feet above the cool water.

Memories of things she wishes undone or unsaid, events she wishes forgotten: small events, simple irritations — the abrasions of propinquity, Roger said once, strangely — indefensible judgements, false starts and disappointments, stillborn things; the recollections circle maddeningly. She watches the play of the cat, the boy happily swinging his legs. Brief infidelities that once amused her. She had encouraged male attention when she shouldn't have. For three years she managed her marriage like a taut rider looking to jump free. If Roger guessed, he'd said nothing.

They had sometimes enacted their helpless love through vital opposition, flesh against flesh. Coming into conflict, body against body — lock of an arm, a gaze. Had she had the courage, she might have left before she'd been steered toward marriage. What could all that matter now?

You step onto the dock, rousing Ydessa from her daydream, a cup of coffee in your hand. You smile, hesitating, then turn to the boy.

Hello, Henry.

He does not reply.

You turn back to Ydessa. Teresa's coming for dinner. Would you like to join us?

Teresa?

Receptionist at the motel. My friend.

Oh. That's sweet of you. No.

You nod. You want your solitude.

No —. Well, yes. I'd be terrible company.

A short silence ensues, save for the quiet rub of Henry's hands against his legs.

This little white cottage — you point to it but Ydessa does not turn — years ago, so I was told, a barrier of birch trees on the other side of the lake caught fire and came folding forward like a book of paper matches. You've seen matches do that?

Yes.

This was about three kilometres from here. I was told that scores of rabbits were roused, tumbling into the air, barking like dogs. Must have been incredible. My father set about hauling what birch could be saved and built this little cabin out of the scorched wood.

A cluster of dogs suddenly begins to howl along the waterfront. Ydessa turns, too sharply, and a spray of Scotch flies from her glass.

Oh. Fuck. Sorry. Clumsy.

Henry twists around.

You two women, heads now bent, observe the spill and the rising smell of booze, say nothing. You turn away.

She watches Barri go, her long legs lifting over rock and flowerbed with uncanny ease. She wonders whether Barri is a lesbian, whether Teresa might be her lover, what it would mean to be lesbians in Bancroft, how they would be treated. Well, it would be an outrage;

she sees that it would be. Barri is too good-looking. Here at Baptiste she and Teresa might pull off a discreet romance, here where for hours at a time no one passes, except by canoe. The heat is rising and soon she will find it unbearable. Overcome and wretched, she finishes her Scotch, staring at the water, and when she is finally thoroughly unhinged, she rises angrily, unsteadily, and climbs the slope to the cottage, leaving Wilson and Henry to ponder the minutiae of the day.

The most famous story concerning master Japanese artist Seeshu is the one which tells of his youth as an unruly boy whose instructor, in exasperation, ties him to a temple post, whereupon the boy cries bitter tears. Using his tears as ink he draws a rat in the dust so realistic that it comes to life, gnaws the ropes, and sets him free.

It is afternoon. Ydessa pulls a tissue from a box and blows her nose. In the mirror, a startling face: hers. She leans in and examines its grotesque proportions, eyes rimmed in red, skin blotchy and pale. The boy stands waiting. An unopened bottle of Scotch sits on the sideboard next to a vintage ashtray. Wildflowers in a pink glass vase release their woodsy perfume. She pulls back from the mirror, opens the bottle with an aggressive twist, pours two fingers into a small juice glass, downs them.

What was that you just drank? the boy asks.

Glenlivet.

What's that?

Booze.

Are you going to drink more booze?

I don't know yet.

Do you drive your car when you drink booze?

Sometimes.

Were you drinking booze two weeks ago?

Jesus.

She moves to the door that leads into a short hall. The boy stands where he is, waiting. She returns holding a map.

As you were so inclined to draw me a map the other day, can you look at this one and tell me where we are and where Millionaire's Island is, relative to where we are?

What does relative mean?

In relation to.

Like, near or far?

Yes.

The boy goes to the window that overlooks the lake.

Millionaire's Island is over there. Near.

Ydessa goes to the window and stands beside the small creature. Having been helpful, he is smiling broadly. She looks out in the direction of his raised finger. Where?

Where the sun path ends.

Sun path.

Yes. He looks up at Ydessa to see if his helpfulness has registered.

Listen, let's go down to the dock again. I'll try to be more hospitable. Come share some digestive biscuits and cheese with the widow.

The boy's happiness vanishes. He looks away.

I understand how it's a widow. I understand that word.

Wilson comes to the back door and the boy lets him in. The cat sits immediately at his feet, tail switching across the floorboards. Ydessa is fetching another two fingers. The boy observes her profile in the mirror, seeing her reflected image as an other, a third presence, a woman arrested in the glass for that moment only: secretive, less certain, taciturn. She moves and the image falls away.

She fills a small tray with cheese and biscuits, a plastic tumbler with orange juice. The boy holds the screen door open for her and they descend to the chairs on the dock facing the lake, its hanging and floating suns. The sun is misted, an Impressionist painting, the forms of shore and wave a wet transience of blurred pink and lavender. She cuts a piece of soft cheese, loads it onto a biscuit, and hands it to the boy, then puts her thumb and index finger into her mouth and makes a sucking sound.

Don't you think it strange that we don't know each other's name?

I'm Henry Rattle. Barri already told you my name.

She ignores his logic. Well, how do you do, Henry. I'm Ydessa Bloom.

The boy looks carefully at her.

Why are you drinking booze, Ydessa?

Look, I left the bottle up there. She waves her hand loosely in the direction of the cottage.

I can't stay much longer.

What's the big hurry?

He had arrived at nine and what is it now? Four o'clock? She pushes an entire biscuit into her mouth and holds it there, her eyes rolling in mock astonishment.

Henry laughs. I know that's rude.

He watches as Ydessa prolongs her chewing, regards her in silence as she rotates her jaw in slow, exaggerated motion, just as a clown might exaggerate eating. At last she swallows.

When it comes to food and drink, I am as rude as it gets. I have the biggest appetite in the kingdom. My god is my *belly*.

Henry understood this with difficulty.

You are very skinny. Are you going to have cheese with your biscuit, or only a biscuit?

No cheese. She looks away. Henry's biscuit lies untouched on the arm of his chair.

Will you keep drinking after I'm gone?

Now who's rude? There's one thing Baba knows, and she never stops saying it. What is this indiscriminate belabouring of a point, Henry?

She gets up from her chair and moves to the edge of the dock to watch the light play on the water. The man and his son fishing from a canoe.

A swarm of blackflies has amassed behind and above her head and neck, but she is oblivious to it. Henry observes their flight patterns. He removes his fountain pen from his back pocket, takes off the cap, and with its tip held high in the air, charts the frenetic impulses of the tiny bodies. Against the sky next to Ydessa he sees an intricate living map, imagines lines of black ink flowing restlessly. This is not the first time he has drawn movements of the world behind the back of an oblivious adult. He recaps his pen, returns it to his back pocket, sits still, hands cupped in his lap.

In his front pocket, Henry has a sapphire ring. The ring had been his mother's. He could not recall ever seeing it on her finger, yet it recalled her to him perfectly. When she died last year, his father packed up all of her things, including the ring, and shipped them off to his aunt. The next time Henry saw his aunt, she gave him the ring, whispering that his mother had wanted him to have it, repeating a puzzling phrase: *Beauty first*.

Don't tell your father, Henry. I'm sorry to be asking you to harbour a secret, but it's for the best. You're too young yet, but, whatever. It was your mother's wish. How can I explain what this ring meant to her? It was our mother's. She was a remarkably beautiful woman. You look a lot like her.

For a year Henry kept the ring in its deep blue velvet case. To ensure its safety, he placed the case in a plastic Easter egg and hid that in a zippered bag his mother gave him for his eighth birthday. Her last gift. That Henry's father would discover the ring has never been a threat. Broken by his wife's death, he no longer enters the places of Henry's life.

For days now Henry has carried the ring in his front pocket, fingering it as he approached Ydessa. His constant worry — his constant compulsion to check for holes in his pocket, afraid he will lose the ring — could not be quelled. He wants to give her the ring. So overwhelmingly does he want this, so strongly has he wished to renew himself in her eyes — he had been the worst anyone could ever be to another, he had almost destroyed her. The ring is all he has to give, yet he resists giving it to her. She is a drinking adult, stealing first a little and then a lot more of the booze that turns adults into strangers.

How come you're not eating?

Henry does not reply. All the tears of his life are rising in him.

I —

Never mind. Please come back another day. I want to be alone now.

I can walk home. He says this to forestall any offer to drive him home. He will not get into her car if she has been drinking booze. He must be careful not to subject himself to violence or force.

It isn't very far. I walk everywhere. I'm a walker.

Well. All right, Henry Walker. See you soon, I expect.

He turns and climbs the cottage drive to the road. His throat aches from holding back tears. He could throw something, a stone or a glass bottle. To keep the tears from spilling, to remember himself and the ring and the road, he names the trees as he runs past: hemlock, maple, sumac, oak.

A small rabbit on the path freezes when she sees him, then leaps away.

Now: with your palms touching, spread your fingers in prayer. Then fold forward, hinging at the hip, letting your hands fall to the ground. *Uttanasana*. With your hands on the ground, float back your legs, keeping your elbows close to your chest, which remains raised above the floor. *Chaturanga Dandasana*. Roll on the tops of your feet, open the chest and straighten your arms. *Urdhva Mukha Svanasana*. Tuck your toes, push back, lift your hips, keeping your arms straight and your shoulders back, relaxed. *Adho Mukha Svanasana*. Jump your feet lightly forward between your hands, straighten the legs and raise your back halfway up, lift your head, then lower your chest to your legs. Uttanasana. Stand up all the way, let your arms fall to your sides, then bring them to prayer. *Samasthitih*.

The body is not a throwaway item, Teresa says. She lowers her knees to her mat, sits back between her heels, arches her sacrum imperceptibly, then slowly curls her spine backward till her torso is outstretched on the floor, arms akimbo. How long it has taken — fifteen years of daily practice — to achieve this pose.

Into the silence of *Supta Vajrasana*, what Teresa calls Lying Thunderbolt, a raven coughs in a high treetop, its one note clear and exact. Sudden light fills the thinking mind.

S I X

SHE STOOD A long time in front of the bottle, then moved away. Everything that could happen between her and Roger *had* happened. How was this possible? She had tried to receive him, take him in, incapable of understanding the nature of the overwhelming love she felt for him and why she had never truly reciprocated his love. Was this true? Yes. A fact. The fact of her past omissions was a torment.

Midnight came on slowly, fog approaching in increments from the far side of the lake, sliding sleuth-like and elusive, as if pausing to assess its own progress. Twenty metres, another twenty. Pause. Wait. She watched the night, grey, now lilac, now violet, the almost-full moon rising behind the scrim of fog, its light breaking up, dispersing, a sailing halo in the violet vapour, shadows breathing. At long last the fog cleared, and a shimmering path of white light split the lake in two.

The pilot of a commercial airline accompanies her to her seat, along the cabin aisle, before returning to the cockpit. The jet roars away from the gate, lifting with ease into the sky, locked and holding to a precise computerized route. From time to time the pilot rises from his seat in the cockpit and visits passengers, serene, jovial, with a grace he makes available to all. He leans over her, speaking profound nonsense, something about a child. He holds a Mason jar that contains blue water. In it many tiny creatures swim. One of the creatures is a child with golden hair. The pilot points to her. Golden light shines round her. The pilot's face is illuminated.

The jar tips, blue water spilling. The girl crawls out and stands. She speaks in strange, elevated, esoteric poetry about true love between two people. Another woman gasps and is immediately shushed. The girl begins to pick at her cheek with an instrument curved at one end like a crochet hook. The hook catches the flesh of her face, which is now loose as an old woman's. She draws flesh away as far as it will stretch then lets it go. Repeats. The passengers sitting closest can hear the slap of saliva in her mouth.

If you want the Truth you must seek it, a man says. A prince leans over the seat to present the dreamer with a Book of Correctives.

Day arrives. She lies on her side, a pillow clutched to her belly, thoughts running skelter as she watches the light slide slowly across the lake, mauve rippling in black water, framed by trees and hills in black shadow, then rippling silver, grey, metallic blue against which lines of branch and leaf became visible. In the distance she can hear the bark of a dog, the high tremolo, faraway claim, of a loon. Rainwater drips close at hand into wet grass. Wilson lies next to her, his small head drifting. Gone. The world beyond the room is now pink and abundant. She lies in a trance, while a line of extraordinary mutating colours parades through and beyond the window. Dinner is hours away.

She thinks she will make inquiries about a boat, a diver. Yes, rent a boat. She half rises from the bed. Wilson opens one eye. She shouldn't try to operate a boat when she is this tired. She drops back down. Wilson dozes.

At noon she rises to make coffee. Henry is outside, sitting astride a fallen log, his body turned away from the kitchen window. Tossing small stones into a green patch of sunlight. The stones make a soft tick against others. *Tick. Tick.* He'll be waiting for a sound from inside the cottage. If she turns on the water, or grinds the coffee beans, he'll know she is there, awake. Has he heard her footsteps? Can he see her, naked at the window, sodden air around her head? She places her right hand on her neck, feels the pulse jump in her jugular. If he were to knock, would she let him in? Maybe he'll get bored, and go away? She could play possum, outlast him, maybe?

She returns to the bed and sits cross-legged on top of the blankets. After a while she experiences a painful contraction in her hips. She crawls under the covers, begins to weep. This cottage is a prison. Henry is only a boy, but he has her locked in. She cries herself to sleep. When she wakes again it is after four in the afternoon, and Henry is gone. She feels ashamed. Something has surged and she failed to climb with it. She has had nothing more to eat than biscuits over many days, is too unsteady to walk or drive. She can't even concentrate enough to read a magazine. Everything is too goddamned much. No TV in the cottage, no radio. If she took a swim she would surely drown. Why do people want to own cottages? It's like being held under water. And yet, how perversely incompetent of her, that she cannot think of a single thing to do. She feels as though her heart is narrowing while her body sags. She has already wept three times this day, but now she releases another flood of tears. Her misery unrelieved.

S E V E N

YOU WERE READING *Pilgrim at Tinker Creek* when Ydessa walked by beneath your window. Where was Henry, who usually accompanied her from morning till night? Oh. There. In the shallows. She is heading toward him, he is pretending to fish.

I am not washed and beautiful, in control of a shining world in which everything fits, Dillard wrote, but instead am wandering awed about on a splintered wreck I've come to care for.

I am no one. Find the zero.

Then two days passed, and Ydessa did not come out of the cottage. Henry came each day, and each day waited faithfully, pitching his stones. From time to time he heard her moving around inside. Sometimes the pump would run for half a minute then stop. He imagined her showering, or making a cup of coffee.

He did not think she would cook. He listened carefully for the sound ice makes when cubes clink against one another in a glass.

The sapphire ring was in his pocket. He felt for holes. He thought about his mother, her wonderful face floating above him in the sky. The pitched stones knocked against each other. Women such as his mother and Ydessa, beautiful, pent up: he could not get near them. The clouds and the sky and the lake are beautiful. When blue is involved, everything is beautiful, otherwise things can be dreary, depressing. Drawing is beautiful. But more than any of his finished drawings, the *act* of drawing is beautiful. Waiting, anticipating — these are terrible. This waiting at Ydessa's back door was like wanting to run in two directions at the same time.

On the third day, late in the afternoon, Ydessa rapped on the windowpane. Henry's head snapped around. She pointed he should go to the side door.

She held the door open, inviting him in. Well, my little soldier.

Henry bent to remove his sneakers. Wilson came into the room and sat down.

First my destroyer, now my sentinel. What gives, Henry Walker?

Henry stood by the door, barefoot, excitement coming alive.

You won't like me asking, but why aren't you in school?

He looked down. How had he not anticipated this? He should have been ready. If he had expected the question, he'd have been ready with a convincing lie. He was flummoxed.

I don't need school.

I see. Ydessa looked at his downturned mouth. You think you have what it takes to forego the rat race?

He bit at a cuticle on his thumb. What's a rat race?

The rat race, my young scholar, is what most people run so as to be able to give something good to loved ones at the end of the day. The rat race is a nasty, all-consuming rut where you eventually stop thinking about loved ones, or about anything, really.

Henry looked up. She was changed. He did not know how, exactly, but she was different. There was fight in her, which was different from the Ydessa who had served him biscuits and orange juice on the dock. She was not drinking at the moment. He came farther into the cottage to an armchair by the window. Wilson followed, his tail high and curling.

My mother died last year, when I was eight. My father is a beekeeper.

I see.

Ydessa crossed the room and sat down opposite Henry in an old rocking chair.

I want to show you something. I've been waiting to show you something.

Okay.

Here. He was standing, reaching into his pocket, taking hold of the ring. He moved toward her and dropped the ring into her opening palm. He stepped back to observe. She didn't say anything, just rocked back and forth in the chair, turning the sapphire this way and that in the light. Her feet were bare. She wore a light summer shift. The tendons in her ankles moved up and down as the balls of her feet pushed against the floor. Blood was rushing into her face now, reddening the skin. Her mouth pursed. She held the sapphire up, partially obscuring her face from full view. Tears streaming down her flushed cheeks. He could not imagine what she was thinking.

Put it on.

She continued to hold the ring aloft.

Inside Henry, in the room where voices gather, a voice was telling him he should not be giving his mother's ring to a stranger, especially not an adult who drank. Do you like it? he asked, to get clear of the voice. She looked at him through her tears but did not reply, only held his gaze. There was comfort in that odd moment as tears continued to drain her heart. He looked at her directly, standing quietly next to her, corners of his mouth downturned. She closed her palm into a fist and clutched the ring to her chest.

It's for you.

There are winds that upbraid us, forty knots for the gale. On water, foam will generate in well marked windrows. On land, small branches begin to break.

I'm very moved, Henry, but I can't accept such a gift.

He faltered. You must. Please try it on. It's a Beauty ring. He took a step forward and placed his small hand on her bare upper arm. When you had your hands on your knees in the ditch and you were rocking back and forth because you were angry, I looked at your finger and the ring was on it. So I know you're the one to give it to.

Bewildering words. He could not elaborate, even when she pressed him. He closed his mouth, tightened his lips, would say no more. She sighed. Slowly, carefully, she placed the sapphire on the ring finger of her right hand. Henry let out a little exclamation of pleasure.

You see? It fits you perfectly.

He lunged toward her, wrapping his arms around her with such happy force that the chair rocketed backward and he slid down into her lap. They both started to giggle.

Henry Walker, it seems you are irresistible.

My name isn't Henry Walker. His words in her lap were a jumble of unintelligible sound. He lifted his face, collecting himself, and stood up. My name is Henry Rattle. He spoke clearly, precisely. I'm nine years old. And I lied about school.

Ydessa laughed.

Henry looked at her, alert. You'll keep it, won't you?

She took his hand.

I won't miss it. He began to plead. I won't miss it because you'll wear it and I'll see it every day.

Ydessa's expression became solemn. As extraordinary as Henry seemed to be, he was a child, innocent of the future. Her inevitable departure could not be clear in his mind. But better not to speak of that now. Better hold her tongue.

Henry Rattle, whatever and whoever you appear to be, you'll be something other, later, and likely you'll change your mind one hundred times.

No, I —

— Stop. Yes, I'll wear it for now.

His happiness sprang into the room, fully returned, and again he dropped into her lap, this time with strength, wrapping his arms tightly around her waist. Hesitantly, she placed a hand on his dirty, tousled hair.

EIGHT

IN THE CITY a person might say, One cappuccino, please, and a tarte Tatin.

I'm sorry, we're just plain folk here.

The neighbourhood fills with a discouraging aggression. You can hear the woman two doors down henpecking her husband, Boyd. You call for Daisy. *Daaaiiisyyy.* Once she's been let in, you linger outside in a sunny patch on a log, playing tic-tac-toe with a wooden match in the dirt below your outstretched legs. A man with Alzheimer's is desperate to find his watch, and everyone knows it. *This is no longer my life!* He accuses the air. A screen door bangs and closes.

Now Ydessa stands above you, asking if there's any place in town that sells challah. I'd make it myself, if I wasn't such a schlemiel.

She drives into town to call Marc. He has said she has to call him every other day. Complaints from clients are piling up. Colleagues are barely competent, he says, to carry her list. When will she be back?

The pay phone is in use. The woman on the phone hopes her listener won't think her filthy as she tells him it was only just this morning she finally drove to the laundromat in town with the flannel sheets with the wonderful reminder of their incredible fucking. Her voice lowers, she cups her hand over the mouthpiece. Filthy. I bought a pillowcase at the thrift shop in town for a quarter, she says. You think I'm cheap. She laughs. The pillowcase is threadbare but the cotton is soft. More, she hopes there's more. Next time, she tells him, better bite your own hand, keep from making such a racket.

The density of a loon's bones allows it to achieve depths unknown to other water birds. So much is still a question about the way loons live that any careful observer may gather new information of scientific value. During a vacation a well-prepared amateur may definitely add to knowledge of the loon by observing even two nesting pairs and recording data about them.

Chicken baked with forty garlic cloves. Late harvest ice wine late on a warm July afternoon. Preheat the oven to four hundred. Rinse and dry the chicken. Place a lemon in the chicken's cavity with a sprig of rosemary and thyme. Truss. Cut off any extra string. Using a small sieve, dust the chicken with paprika. Cook for an hour. Take the rocking chair and a very generous second glass down to the dock and rock while waiting. Watch the sun go red. Here comes Henry.

She can detect a slight change in the noises inside the cottage. She listens to the changes. Her stay at the lake having extended beyond her original intention, she notices old sounds changing into new ones. She pours half a glass of Scotch and knocks it back. Somewhere water drips slowly. Somewhere a tick, somewhere a hum. After a while she stops drinking, goes to bed. A bowl of cream on the floor beside the bed. The sound of Wilson's lapping is strange music to the underground consciousness that pulls her in.

At the beginning of a wave there occurs in Anchorwoman's heart a small event, a single beat, released to the floor of the lake. She wills her heart to stir the sand, let go a foaming wave. Silver, its skin fine as gauze. Sand ripples. Tiny eggs stir. A breeze lifts. Anchorwoman broods. Something trapped.

A charge, released, seeks, ponders. It is true geometry, every wave she bears eventually to become a mirror. Time. Patience. Above the surface a ray of morning sun catches the crown of the highest tree. She is not finished.

How does a golden wing against the sky oblige her?
Revelation. Her wave the lived life of rain. What is the life of the
lake bowl, stream of water flowing in then out, not drained, not
desert, sun not extinguished, lake not ice field, light and branch
hovering, feather adrift? To live the proverb: every vessel makes its
own waves.

Anchorwoman releases waves, but the lake is no longer a
talking cure as in ancient times. Go seek bough. Propulsion begins
in her, a wave is ushered forth, freeing something hidden, the heart
as it seeks, skin warp with subtle threads. Ask a child. Go seek
bough. Wave shivers, heart swells, Anchorwoman comes riding
high as bough breaks, cradle falls.

To hire a boat on Baptiste is not easy. First, you need to prove
you're fit to handle one. When was the last time Ydessa operated a
one hundred horsepower engine? Oh.

Against her wishes, she has to ask Barri. Would you take me
out in your elegant boat?

My father was a master craftsman, you explain as you free the boat
from its moorings, step down into the driver's seat. Daisy jumps
into the back. The lake calm, the day pleasant. You extend your

hand and Ydessa steps down, her weight dropping lightly to the thwarts.

My father built this boat when I was five. Mahogany. It's kept its shape very well.

Both of you seem cheerful, the hurry of Ydessa's thoughts behind her for the time being. She confides that she has made a promise to herself: no more messy days lost inside the cottage. Her slack face in the mirror had filled her with disgust, she says. She thought she'd kept something at bay, but her face had showed all that.

The morning looks well. She speaks to keep her spirits up. What a sky. In my heart there's been a great longing for distances.

For Roger? you ask.

She doesn't know, she doesn't know much. She knows that the life she is living here is compulsion, knee-jerk. Roger would have been made entirely happy by the morning's little adventure. Roger would have rejoiced at the day, the boat, the sky, a new friend. He would have settled into an easy gratitude as they proceeded across the bright water. Ydessa tries to relax into her seat.

The drift, the lift of the boat on the waves, is very pleasant. The tone of the motor is also pleasant, its pitch too. It shuts out subtler sounds coming over the water. You have to shout above the motor's hum. You point. Blueberry Island. Warm channels of sunlight stream down between white clouds. Soft grey shadows fan out overhead like ribs of a celestial rib cage over the waters of this world. The wind sweet and warm. You travel slowly, as Ydessa has requested.

I don't know how to swim. We had a backyard pool, but I never learned. Nervous passenger, too.

You ask her if she likes to be in control. There are those who drive, and there are those who like to be driven.

Like to be in control. Really? What a sorry sap that must show me to be.

You make your way, Ydessa's hand gripping the side of the boat. She withdraws it to her lap. She scans the water for other boats, is she looking for careless boaters who might make trouble? She closes her eyes. Her mind will fall into its mechanical grooves. The vibration beneath her feet causes her again to grip the side of the boat. She opens her eyes, withdraws her hand again to her lap. The ring she is wearing gleams. After a while she places both hands between her thighs.

The sun beats down. The world is green, then blue, moving slowly in its round, on the tip of her tongue are words you want to help her to say: *I'm sorry. I'm frightened.* You travel slowly. She withdraws her hands from between her thighs, for a third time places them in her lap. She fidgets with the ring, which glitters in the sunlight, the stone brilliant. She's watching its colours flare and dance. The water curls into little waves beneath the boat.

The day is warm, its light soft. Ydessa's heart will soon break up like ice.

Questions flow through her. Was she right to send Roger's ashes to his mother in New York? Impetuous. Perhaps she had underrated the value of ritual, had made ritual into a kind of checklist, enacting grief by checking off items on a to-do list. Body? Cremate. Check. Ashes? To Alicia. Check. Mourning? Let a little time pass. Her entire body is clenched, her muscles strained around the delicate tissues of her flesh, her breath short and high in her throat, her groin turned to soft clay, emptiness in her solar plexus, grief stored and twisting in her hips. She catches herself gripping the side of the handsome boat, hand clenched like a baby's around a finger. A kind of fury pulls in her skin. While Roger rolls and turns, while the water beneath her rolls and turns, easily, carefree, she is twisted.

Today you pass through the narrows toward the site where the Cessna fell. You say nothing. In the shallows tall reeds stand quiet, their long shadows undulating like an exquisite dream of laughter. A school of bass flashes in the cool water below, flash, dart, submerge, re-emerge. Daisy is ecstatic. The world below the surface is everywhere instinctual, quick and light. With dexterity you manage the boat, which now stirs long reeds in its easy slide above the loose blue-grey patterns waving over the pebbled lake bottom. In the slide, a shift, and Ydessa's fear becomes unmanageable, no longer a stone she can hold in her palm. You sense the knots tighten within her. The world is becoming too small, the light is hardening.

Let's go back. Can we please turn back?

You reverse and retreat from the narrows. You travel slowly. The sun beats down.

You jump from the boat with the line to moor it. Once it's secured, you offer your hand to Ydessa, who takes it, clearly grateful for this small kindness.

Thank you.

Daisy drops her head to lick Ydessa's bare calf.

In the evening, you write a note on old family stationery, slip it into an envelope and quietly tack it to the back door of the cottage. *You are going through something difficult, trying to sort things out. I understand. You need time. As far as I am concerned there is no hurry. Stay here as long as you like. I hope you won't think me impertinent, but Teresa teaches yoga three times a week in town.*

*Perhaps you would find the classes beneficial. Teresa says the body is
a paradise. If I understand her correctly, she means that the body
contains what we might otherwise mindlessly give away. There is a class
tomorrow. Shall I tell Teresa you'll attend? Fondly, Barri*

Lake is a basin. Night's basin is a black bowl in which stars float. A
loon rounds slowly through the stars, the unbounded bowl, which
carries her like a lost ship. Her black sail mirrors a sister-cry that
sounds far out beyond the quiet shoreline.

Dreams commence.

One woman's life is bound up in the foam and wave of lakewater,
in fine grains of sand that she carries each day in her hand, past
evergreens, past ancient white and jack pine and a vast oak of
unknown age that sprawls on the shoreline, her living unassailable
by earthbound dangers, her life protected by green boughs lit by
the rising sun, her silhouette brazen against silver skies. She might
be a comfort station to one bereaved and bereft. When boughs do
break, when day must break then break again. When on waking the
ego is thrown against Self to regain this sweet Baptiste, wave upon
wave of new light falling, to pause on shore before drawing out
again; when a stranger appears, unexpected but happily received,
and her host spreads a cloth on a table set beneath fast-fading

blooms, gold dropping gold, blood of the sun: treasure. Splendour.
Dust on the cloth for gold that remains, glittering shapes hovering,
eye melting, bees zooming.

Ydessa woke the next morning, head pounding. Nausea filled her,
a sour snaking sickness that rose again and again from her belly to
the base of her throat. She stood at the window. Henry saw her,
came to the door and spoke, his voice muffled.

Here's an envelope for you.

YOU WERE WORKING in your garden, estimating growth and rain.

I got your note, she says.

You did.

I mean — yoga. What's it all about? That, say, running isn't about. For example.

Yoga asks different questions.

Questions.

It's a philosophy as well as exercise. You might find it engaging.

Well, I'll see if I can fit it into my busy schedule.

Teresa sits on a white bath towel in a small candlelit studio, before a group of six women, two rows of three, also sitting on towels, legs straight out in front, upper bodies angled forward from their hips. The pull in Ydessa's lower back is a torment. *Paschimottana-sana*. Forward fold. Two women touch their noses to their knees.

What you are seeking is spaciousness. Breathe into the space the pose creates. When you breathe, you create new space, new awareness in the body, and as new space is created, old grooves and habits of thought burn away. You are de-structuring and you are restructuring, both simultaneously. We chastise ourselves: no longer flexible, no longer beautiful, no longer wily, just old women fit for the trash heap. Never enough of a woman, we say, and now it's too late. By the time we get to middle age, most of us want to become less of a child, shuddering, overwhelmed before life's difficulties. I've done some work, but I can't teach you how. Not really. All I can do is share with you the postures of yoga.

Ydessa lets up a little on her forward fold to grab a look at Teresa, now in full Paschimottanasana, head and upper body resting on her outstretched legs, arms fully extended along the floor. How pompous. What's Teresa got to crow about? She's a smoker, for god's sake.

In the sunlight that pours like liquid into the studio, the hairs on Teresa's bare arms shine long and dense. The skin on both her forearms is scored and marked, scarred as if a rake had been drawn across them. Ugly, Ydessa all but thinks, though the word doesn't quite arrive, a small catch unnoticed in her breast.

Prepare yourselves for final relaxation. If you want an eye pillow, place a hand on your belly and I'll bring you one. This final pose is called *Savasana*. Corpse pose. All other poses are in preparation for Savasana, for full relaxation.

Ydessa is stretched out on her back, demoralized, quietly furious. Corpse pose!

Teresa fiddles with a tape deck until she finds the music she wants. The studio fills with the sound of ocean waves, the high call of shorebirds. The spaces between the women's bodies diminish: the rustlings, the sighs, the shifting lessens, as each woman settles onto her towel and begins to relax first toes, then feet, calves, knees, thighs, buttocks, sacrum, and groin — Teresa says groins and Ydessa corrects her silently. It's *groin*. Get the grip.

Relax your spine, your shoulders, and your neck. Relax your mouth, your teeth, your lower jaw. Relax your eyes and the skin around your eyes. Relax your brow. Relax your forehead. Relax your skull and the space around your ears.

Voodoo, Ydessa almost thinks, though the word — clumsy — will not quite shape itself. Ridiculous, she does think, not anticipating the small latch in her breastbone that has clicked, releasing a flood of tears that flows up through a network of spaces like steps, and spills and spills and spills.

They had made a kind of furious love, and Roger had shouted wildly before falling back in a grimace onto the bed, frightening her. As she lay in the dark among the tangled sheets, listening, disbelieving, a pillow pressed roughly to her pelvis, he told her at last about his other lovers.

Jonathan got sick, many others got sick. Jonathan's white blood count was dangerously low. He'd been bleeding for two days from his anus, the blood watery and thin. They admitted him to Bellevue on First Avenue. These were medical mysteries then, you understand, many doctors were resistant. Some began to think that such cases were already dropping off. I called Keith, we came to the hospital to help Jonathan. We stayed with him, no sleep for forty-eight hours, and every time he felt an urge to shit — he had these ongoing urges to shit, but there was no shit, he was absolutely void — we'd lift him up ourselves, nurses nowhere to be seen. We'd raise him from the bed and lower him onto a cold porcelain bedpan. These are impossible to keep warm. His bowels would move a half cup of blood. One of us would change the sheets if he'd bloodied them. We'd lift him away from the pan, wipe his ass with a damp cloth, put him back on the bed. One of us would wash out the pan. We'd take it to the bathroom and pour the blood into the toilet bowl. We weren't careful, you see, we didn't have any idea at that time what the cost could be, holding his blood in our hands. What the cost was. It was foolishness, and we laughed. Yes, we actually laughed. He wanted shit and got blood instead, and we stood over him, his blood in the pan, all three of us laughing. Finally the urge to shit lessened then stopped. All he was at the end: just bone and laughter. His skin was like alabaster against the white cotton sheets. Like marble. He was as beautiful as any Michelangelo, emptied of blood. He said, Roger, lift me up in the bed. And then he was gone.

After a minute's silence she reached across his naked body to turn on the light.

Why are you turning on the light?

I need to see your face. I need to see the face of the man who waits this long to tell the woman set to marry him that he's HIV positive, and gay.

No, sweetheart. Not gay. Not positive. No. Nothing's changed. It's the very same face, belonging to the very same man who's anxious to marry you. Though yours, I must say, is utterly different at the present moment.

He studied her in the soft light.

Utterly different.

———

Every woman needs the luxury to fail. Every woman at the threshold of a new experience in the world is given to paralysis. Yoga teaches us to breathe across the threshold.

She was holding the posture known to practitioners as downward dog, Adho Mukha Svanasana, holding and yet not holding the position, a new and paradoxical concept that wanted thinking about. She tried to turn off her mind but didn't know how. The manoeuvre seemed impossibly difficult for a position that looked so graceful. Other postures had been introduced: cat tilt, eagle, crow and side crow, moon and half moon, until the studio became a forest of symbol and effort. Her heart pounded. Her head hung upside down, blood thumped. In Adho Mukha Svanasana, bodies form more or less the arch of a children's game, London Bridge is Falling Down. She thought of that game, its collapse and giggle, as she struggled to hold the pose, uncertain, straining, trying to breathe, her heart so full that the sound of a raven's sudden deep cough overfilled it and she began again to cry, tears pooling on the studio floor. Teresa observed the pool. Again the call of the bird rocked the studio. In a posture called child's pose she let out a single wild sob. If anyone had moved to touch her, she would have broken down completely. No one touched her. No one moved. The room was still.

The yoga tradition makes the declaration, All is painful, all is transient. That we can feel grief and pain; that we can know more grief and pain is ahead of us. Our bodies are perishable, we will have to face death; any meaning we have found in life will, at life's end, be forgotten; birth and death alike create despair. We hate life, because life ends. What is the point of such a pointless existence? This is the problem yoga addresses.

A robin lands on the studio window.

This problem captures in essence the spirit of our age. When was the last time you discussed this problem with a friend?

Questions flow through her. She thinks of the cottage and its wide lake, of people she is meeting there, their strange, bright welcome. Barri's extreme kindness. More than four weeks have passed. She is starting to get involved in the things of this town. Not smart. She has been able to put off her boss, but for how much longer?

She meditates on the puzzle of grief. Why is she so passively allowing odd little Henry to accompany her here and there? The days accumulate without direction. Every morning Barri takes Henry and Ydessa out in the old mahogany boat. Some mornings the mist on the lake is so thick they can't see the shoreline opposite. She drinks strong coffee from the thermos that Barri unfailingly supplies. While sipping black coffee she notes small patterns the rising sun paints on the water's ebb and flow and on the birch trees hugging the shore. Barri doesn't disturb her meditations. Tuned to some alternative frequency, Henry draws his strange equations.

On Monday and Wednesday mornings she takes yoga classes at Teresa's studio, on Sundays she attends an evening practice. Between classes she loiters, roams aimlessly, through slack, restless hours. Everything adrift. She thinks she might be dangerously depressed, knows she has become irresponsible. She has not asked Barri to look for the place where Roger's plane crashed, hasn't asked anyone why it crashed, whether the trouble was with the plane or, perhaps as likely, with the pilot. This torpor seems to illustrate what she has always been at base: a dreamer. She is losing momentum. Questions she's denied for years, secrets she has kept, begin to rock her. She draws her mind back to her breath, as Teresa instructs. The mind is a bucking bronco.

Henry bursts through the cottage door shouting, Kittens at the lodge!

A stray tabby and her five kittens have been discovered beneath the floorboards of the laundry cabin. A staff member placed food in a sheltered place and the mother has begun to take it. Now the staff want homes for the kittens. She has avoided the lodge, avoided even walking along the road past its drive, taking instead the higher road that leads to the small café and store. Now Henry coaxes her there.

They approach the cats quietly, Ydessa's heart filling with an unfamiliar tenderness for the mother, who creeps out from under the cabin and hunkers down a few metres away, observing them, a kind of beseeching in her unblinking yellow eyes. The kittens bat one another with graceless paws or bite their mother on the soft fur of her raised white chin. Almost a kitten herself, she displays forbearance. The scene is as lovely as any Ydessa has ever seen.

You must take her. Henry points to the mother.

What?

You must keep her.

But what about Wilson?

Henry looks at the tabby, his expression open and vast. She'll be Wilson's happiness. He looks at her, imploring.

I —

I can help you care for her. It's easier to find a kitten a home. Anyone will take a kitten, because they are nice. But the mother needs you.

The tabby lies on her side as the kittens nudge against her, purring loudly.

I can't, Henry. I just can't.

The class over, she is free to go. Her mind free-associates.

Henry.

Someone should put that kid under wraps, she thinks. Put him in a climate-controlled vitrine, preserve him for two hundred years. Never allow such a spirit to be snuffed out by other people's inattention.

Teresa stands at the door of the small change room, disrupting Ydessa's reverie. There is Ydessa, alone, in bra and underpants, her fine body vulnerable and crystalline, almost translucent. Teresa could have wept. How thin she is. How much thinner will she allow herself to get? Teresa knows something about the appeal of self-obliteration. She doesn't speak.

I was thinking rather sentimentally just now about Henry Rattle. Ydessa laughs. She turns her back and steps into her cotton dress. Sometimes I do things, uncontrolled, reckless things. In the studio, in Savasana, my body wants to go on and on doing nothing. I don't understand yoga.

She turns around and gives Teresa a weak smile.

Barri tells me I'm a driver not a passenger. You can't drive yoga, though, right? Isn't yoga all about killing off the desire for control?

Teresa studies Ydessa's rapidly shifting gaze. Just going through the motions, she thinks. Just mechanical. Ydessa makes a quick gesture, as if to pick up her bag, as if to leave the room. She pulls back in the middle of the gesture and straightens, her eyes filling with tears.

I'm so fucking lost, and I don't know where to go. I don't want to go home, and I can't stay here.

She is a stream of heat. She looks directly at Teresa, who returns her gaze. They stand like that for some time.

Standing there, thin and alarmed, unfastened, lit from within, her tears glistening, wet on her bone-bright cheeks. Teresa does not speak, won't speak. To speak would be to limit the sixty-five directions into which Ydessa might at this moment step. She wonders how the unconscious continues to deny so dramatically what pulls at Ydessa. Her nights fill with dreams, perhaps.

The world is round. Ydessa's tears subside. Teresa says nothing. She puts out her hand, cups Ydessa's chin and cheek with her palm. Ydessa has never before looked so deeply into the eyes of another human being. She smiles nervously and the spell is broken. She turns her eyes to the floor. Teresa removes her hand, gesturing to Ydessa — time to dress and go.

———

The world is round and its ways are many, but to Ydessa the way is blighted. A diver is unavailable. Everything about life with Roger had been. . . . The sentence is already an illusion. No consistency, all is transient. Try again. When Roger was alive. A false oracle, for doesn't he prowl near her to this day? Going on alone, but where? There has never been a time she didn't know she was alone in life. But why know it so irrepressibly now? When Roger was alive. A thought that repeats, defers her own truth, divides her from the grief of remembrance, from the deepest kind of sorrow for an unloved life.

Why will he not knock? Why does he stay in the grass back of the cottage, conscious of every move I make in here, wanting to be with me and not knocking?

The August morning began as so many had — glorious, the clouds lazy, scent of pine needles in damp earth slowly rising, sweet pungency. Cottage windows still open as they had been throughout the night. Morning with no impediment. In ten minutes Barri will leave her kitchen with a thermos of hot coffee and greet Henry coming to her with his notebook, his crooked smile, and One, two, three, Ydessa! They will call out to her, laughing. When she is ready all three will descend together to the dock and untie the boat, exchanging smiles, speaking very little, just Can you hold this? Do you have your pen? Are you settled? Everyone ready? She'll make effort to smile, even though she has a hammering headache. She'll make effort to be, if not glad of the morning, at least present, trying to keep her hangover a secret from Henry.

She renews her glad friendship in silence, in sunlight. This is how it is. Barri controls the boat, Ydessa controls her tongue, Henry draws the rolling patterns of the fluctuating world. *When Roger was alive.* The sentence won't come alive. It goes nowhere. *Always been alone* is quite possibly the most pompous thought she's ever had. Anguish over her sustained indolence — could it shift, could indolence be redefined as patience? Has there ever been a time when she was free not to act? Must a woman who contrives not to act punish herself with the visible, tangible world?

She has no security system there. She could at any time be attacked in her bed at night by thieves or rapists or murderers.

Rose.

A savage lakeside place she knows nothing about. It contains fish: this is all she knows. Fish for a fish-crazy husband.

Rose. Please. You underestimate Ydessala.

I'm not thinking of our daughter. I'm thinking about the night, the shuddering and moaning in the dark. The evil schemes when a man is hot with blood. The cottage should have an alarm system. Ydessa told me she keeps the doors and windows unlocked. What kind of lady is this landlady next door? No phone, should Ydessa need to call the 911. Not even a TV. Not a microwave. And now this cult leader Ydessa learns yoga from. Ydessa is *meshuga*, she is weak in her choices. Weak. Why is she so weak, Sam? I'll tell you why.

No, Rose. Stop now. I don't want to hear.

She is too much with strangers, is why. She has always been too much with strangers. She was too much with strangers, and Roger —. A mother knows things. It is better for Ydessa that she is without him.

Rose. Please. Stop.

A severed arm with black veins drifting in the shallows where the little ponies feed. One pony noses it gently. Darts away. Returns to nose it again. Darts. Two gather, then three, a small school, which encircles and noses the strange sliding thing. Bloody ligaments, like a soft red ladder dragging, its lowest rung catching and rotating serenely in the rolling silverleaf and redbud.

Zebra mussels siphon detritus waving on the sandbar.

Time passes.

Teresa arrives unannounced with a picnic lunch. From the small shed next to the dock she brings out an old wooden table and four chairs. Why four? We'll invite Ydessa and Henry.

She sets a linen cloth over the table and with a gesture like a magician's sleight of hand makes appear out of her picnic basket four white china plates, glassware, linen napkins, and a bouquet of the orange wildflowers known as Indian paintbrush. Tabouli and hummus, falafels, a Greek salad, an exotic tea, one tomato sandwich wrapped in wax paper — for Henry, who likes tomatoes straight out of a can and is now promised the splendour of a ripe Ontario beefsteak tomato on plain white bread.

At the end of the meal Teresa reaches across the table to pour jasmine tea into Ydessa's cup, its perfume dusky and murky. Why jasmine tea? Why tabouli? Why not chicken, Ydessa thinks, chicken with cold white wine, like normal picnickers? Why aspire to some Eastern version of a picnic? Teresa's need to infuse the mundane with traditions from the East is a bit dubious. Yoga and the scent of jasmine. Please.

Henry asks if Barri would please read aloud from *The Sword in the Stone*, a reading she began one evening when it seemed nothing else could be done to persuade him to go home.

I *will* read to you. But first *you* will take a bar of soap, and shampoo, into the lake with you and have a lovely bath.

He looks at her like maybe she is unwell.

A bath? In the lake?

Right.

He doesn't argue, but his movements turn devastating, slow and drawn out as mime. He rises, pulls his pants down, steps out of these. Looks up at Barri.

Throw them into the water, Henry.

He raises his eyebrows. Into the water?

Yes.

The pants sink slowly.

Now your underwear. And your shirt.

Barri watches him, she is breathing quickly but her face is neutral.

He undresses fully, he gestures — into the lake, too?

She nods.

Now get in. Use the ladder. The water will be like silk. It'll be wonderful.

She rises to retrieve soap, shampoo, and a towel from the shed and does not see him as he descends the ladder, trembling. Discomposed. Teresa says to him, That's right, Henry.

With shampoo and soap in hand, Barri gets down on her knees at the edge of the dock and instructs him, step by step. Dip your head. Dip it again. Here, take the bar of soap and lather it in your hands. Now give it back to me while you soap your neck, arms, torso.

He looks up, uncertain.

Where your heart is, and all around it, down to your belly.

He does as she asks.

Now lather the rest.

He is puzzled.

All of you. Everything. Front and back. Sit here on the ladder. We three will turn our backs. Once you've soaped up everywhere, go back in the water for a rinse.

When they hear the splash from his dive, Barri turns again and says, Climb up on the ladder and I'll shampoo your hair.

His small body, shivering, as she works the shampoo right down to his scalp, sculpting a hilarious froth.

Okay, she says, when it's clear that he will never relax into the massage. Step down and dive like a dolphin, and dive again, and again.

And again.

Good.

She asks Teresa to go up to the house to fetch one of her shirts and a sweater.

What about my own clothes? he wants to know.

Not sure. We'll think about them later. They'll be all right in the lake for now. Okay. Step up here and I'll towel you down just like a trainer towels a boxer. Wasn't that the most glorious bath you've ever had?

He is mute, but shining.

Barri reads twenty pages of the book, there on the dock, while the treetops shimmer in reflected light, the four of them dappled through the slant branches of the trees.

Henry speaks at last. Read Merlyn's part again, about the thing no one can take from you.

She flips back a few pages.

The best thing for disturbances of the spirit, replied Merlyn, beginning to puff and blow, is to learn. That is the only thing that never fails. You may grow old and trembling in your anatomies, you may lie awake at night, listening to the disorder of your veins, you may miss your only love and lose your moneys to a monster, you may see the world around you devastated by evil lunatics, or know your honour trampled in the sewers of baser minds. There is only one thing for it then — to learn. Learn why the world wags and what wags it. That is the only thing the poor mind can never exhaust, never alienate, never be tortured by, never fear or distrust, and never dream of regretting. Learning is the thing for you.

Learning *is* the thing, especially for you and me, Ydessa, Henry says.

Why especially me?

Because you lie awake, you miss your love, you lost your monkeys, and every day you call the world names.

It's moneys, not monkeys. And I haven't! I don't!

Teresa laughs. Yes you do. Henry's right.

Well, hasn't the world earned some name-calling? Isn't it going to hell in a handbag?

You mean handbasket, Teresa says.

Barri looks at them over the rim of her cup. How long has it been since a table has been set for more than Teresa and herself? And now this precocious child, at last clean, by her hand, his misery forgotten for now, interested in a wide array of ideas and things, marked by his appetite for inquiry. Going to teach Ydessa a lesson.

Explain what you mean, Henry.

He looks away from the table, to the treetops overhead. Learning is important. Merlyn says the world wags, like a dog wags its tail. My father says the world is made up of fools and beggars.

Fools today, wise ones tomorrow, Barri says. Because I've seen that whatever is true of the world now with time will become otherwise true, and something else will take its place.

Ydessa scoffs. You say that because you think this little planet of ours isn't broken beyond all repair.

Barri laughs. I say this for Henry's sake. May you align yourself, Henry, with those who make effort to keep the world from becoming some superficial idea a few scientists hope to prove.

Henry says, I am learning words today, Barri, but what do they mean? This proves how learning is the thing for me, and not from a dictionary either.

Ydessa stands. Merlyn is magical, his knowledge is magical. This is only a nice story. None of us will ever in this life find a teacher as wise as him. He lives backwards in time while the rest of us have to crawl forward, stupid as clams. I'm going up to pee. Can I bring anything down from the house?

After she is out of hearing range, after Henry has gone looking by the side of the big house for Wilson, Teresa stands.

She'll drink something. She thinks we have no idea. Whenever she's unsettled she has to drink.

Henry returns, disappointed, takes his seat at the table. After looking at him for a while, Barri lifts her spoon and Henry's empty glass, places them before him on the table and carefully fills each with water from the pitcher.

Which is more full of water, Henry, spoon or glass?

He looks from one to the other. The thinking his mind conducts is evident, bright as sun on water. Sometimes the patterns of his thinking, he thinks, are worth a drawing. He pulls the cap from his fountain pen and makes a brief sketch in his little book.

May I see that? Barri leans toward him once he is finished.

He pushes the book along the table till it lies open in front of her.

She scrutinizes the drawing for a long time. Teresa begins to clear the table and Henry moves away to the edge of the dock.

May I have this? she asks.

He turns and shrugs. I guess so.

How would you like me to remove it from your book?

Just take the book. I can ask my father to get me another one.

She frowns. There's no need to make sacrifices in order to seem generous.

Sacrifices?

You'd lose all your drawings to give me just one drawing.

Teresa is stacking dirty dishes onto a tray. Here, Henry, take this knife and cut out the drawing Barri wants.

He places the little book upright on the table, takes the knife from Teresa, holds the book and the knife, one in each hand, considering. He puts them down.

I want you to take the whole book. I don't want to wreck it.

I will *not* take the whole book. Deprive you of all your observations? Too much. You show me the drawing whenever I ask you, all right?

Yes. All right.

And when you're ready to let it go, I'll buy the whole book.

Buy it? How much will it cost? He rises and places the pen in his back pocket, keeping his eyes fixed on hers.

Sky's the limit. You name your price.

Barri, the sky is a huge place.

Well, that's it, then. Huge price. Shall we go for a boat ride when Ydessa comes down from the cottage?

Henry smiles. The day will move on. What if day could move backwards, as Merlyn's days had done? He has an image for day moving backwards: he pictures it above the dock. He makes like he is still holding his pen, and draws the image against the sky. He opens to the latest page of his book, comparing that drawing to the one he just made.

Ydessa is back. Were they waiting for her to make their next step? Half complaint, half pleasure. Well, what are you waiting for? On such a lovely afternoon as this, shouldn't we be fishing?

Henry lets out a whoop.

I know where the poles are. He is already running toward the house. I know where the worms are.

The women can hear him as he throws open the door of the mudroom and enters, to wrestle with poles and life jackets. How deep is Barri's wish that this summer will never end. Once Ydessa departs, whatever could she do to shield Henry from inevitable anguish, joy foundered?

To prolong the moment, seized by longing, she'll paint in an effort to record the splendid afternoon. She shouts up the path. Just bring three poles, Henry! I'm not going.

They can hear his muffled consent. She turns. Teresa, will you drive the boat?

What? Me?

Yes, you. I want to paint. You three go fishing. I'll stay back this once.

Ydessa lowers herself into her usual seat in the boat. Once settled, she looks up at Teresa, and laughs. Is there anything you can't do?

Teresa smiles down at her. She doesn't really mean it. Ydessa isn't envious of Teresa, not at all. But at this moment, all of them are equally intoxicated.

―――――

As they drift, lines slack in the lake's afternoon stillness, Henry tells them things he is learning about the sun from a book his father lets him read at night in bed. How light takes time to travel. When I look at your face, Ydessa, I see it in the past, because light takes a little bit of time to travel to my eyes. Everything in front of us takes time to reach our eyes. When we catch our fish, it will be in the past, because to see it will take a little bit of time. When we look at the stars at night, some are probably dead, it takes so long for starlight to reach us. Some stars died a long time ago, but their light keeps falling down on us. The sun is a star. Every single day the sun is getting a little bit hotter. Unless scientists figure out a way to move Earth farther away from the sun, soon it will be too hot for people to live here.

How soon? Ydessa asks, watching her line become suddenly taut.

Two billion years. How long is that?

Teresa sees Ydessa's line jerk, and says, Long enough to catch this fish. Hold steady, Ydessa! The good news, according to Henry — this fish won't be quite cooked by the time you haul it in!

TEN

ROGER'S NAKED BODY on a marble table in the centre of a cold room. A portcullis stands closed on one wall, a small window with iron grill on a second, a marble fireplace and mantel on a third. The dreamer has been standing for hours.

Exhausted by the death watch, in a sudden heavy swoon she slides down the fourth wall to lie twisted at its base, unable to rise. Unconscious.

Soon bells ring out, rousing her. Roger's body has disappeared while she slept, and in its place on the marble table are bubbles, vaporizing, Roger's mouth speaking from within each bubble, uttering sounds within the iridescence as one by one the bubbles pop. Then a sudden, clear utterance.

It's blue here, like a swimming pool. You can come here, my love.

A great force takes hold of the dreamer, twisting her, elongating muscles, wringing fibres, pulling her out and away from the body no longer fully occupied, now limp like a rag doll, slumped on the floor. Roger's voice chants, a drone, clear but receding. *You can come here.* An incubus, an irresistible force: to lift with it and go, like a frog sucked out of its skin. Then — in the fight of her life against the force, the pull to abandon her body, cleaving to her own flesh in ancient bondage to living, drawing on an opposed, a downward force, she resists the irresistible, flesh ripping, wet suit of skin and sinew tearing away, clay heart bursting, flying, and a great wailing begins.

Four in the morning, the August moon pours its thin stream of molten pewter across the lake. Wolf hour, hour of the dead. More human beings die at four in the morning than at any other time of day. To wake at four unnerves her.

At six o'clock she rises to make a cup of strong coffee. A pink mist envelops the lake.

On the shore of Baptiste Lake, in early morning light cascading serenely from the tops of trees, you gather kindling for the wood stove, nannyberries and cranberries for the green bowl. Tomorrow, berry blood on paper, some trace of wave significance, brush of red oil, drawn from its dwelling place, a secret seeking its moment, risen within a fallen cradle that rides an inbound wave, a wheel to draw one round.

Many mornings, as Ydessa sips her coffee at the front windows, movement on the dock catches her eye. A great blue heron, stepping slowly, purposefully across it. The heron will fish from the rocks, holding its elegant body impossibly still. If she moves too quickly to find a less obstructed view, it will turn from its hunt, all grace, and lift into the sky.

Movement. Henry, standing on the dock, his hand held aloft, drawing the grid of sky raked by pink clouds, small conductor in jeans and T-shirt, tracing, in intricate detail, the transcendent rays of early light. She watches him without tiring. If Henry were hers, she thinks, suddenly seized by feminine tenderness, she'd lay down her life for him.

She leaves the window, pours a second coffee, goes down to the dock. Wilson accompanies, clearing the grasses in short leaps.

Hello, Henry. Awfully early, isn't it?

I got up early and came over. We could go over to the lodge and get one of those kittens.

His right eye begins to twitch.

Maybe you're thinking I wouldn't properly care for a kitten.

She has to admit that the thought did cross her mind.

I understand, because I'm instar, like a caterpillar. An instar is the time between the times a caterpillar loses its fur. You would rather have a kitten than the mother, because a kitten has longer to live.

She sips her coffee, watching him begin to tell what he is here to say.

I find little caterpillar skins in the grass. I could show you. A caterpillar splits its skin many times.

She considers a caterpillar crawling out of its skin. So right now is instar for you?

He puts away his pen, sits down in one of the deck chairs, looks up at her, his eye twitching furiously. He bites his lip.

After the accident —

Nobody got hurt.

— I decided I would give you my mommy's ring. I was waiting for the right time. It was a little bit hard to wait. I saw that you were a drinking person — He stops. Now I've given you the ring.

She sits down in the other chair.

Is something losing its fur?

He nods. His head falls back against the deck chair, his gaze wandering among the swaying treetops. His tears fall.

I don't think you'll come back. From where you're going.

Where am I going?

He sits up straight to flick the drops from his cheeks.

I know where your husband's arm is.

Pardon me?

This is a shock, the words *husband* and *arm* on Henry's lips. She has told no one what she'd seen when Roger's shroud was lifted. It was too grotesque — his left arm severed, a pale limb lost, the left side of his body a blood-dark quarry of veins and guts.

Words storm her. She is dizzy, she might faint.

I walked along the road last night. I sat a long time in the ditch. I wanted to stay there till the stars came out. I wanted to see the evening star, but I couldn't. Little clouds came. I wanted to come over here and ask if I could stay with you. I know you won't let me. My dad doesn't like me to talk about you. I never said anything to him about you and me that day.

She repeats, Nobody got hurt.

Last night I took my secret path, and I sat on the beach, piling up the feldspar stones I can find there. At first I thought it was a little black log.

Okay, Henry, that's enough.

To pay a diver to find Roger's arm, thinking that finding it might also secure, not the past, not even a doubtful love, but *something*, a direction maybe, some forward momentum. The reclamation to be *hers*. In her fantasy it was *she* who found the courage to locate the arm, and, more importantly, the hand. She was to be the one, not this ill-kempt, neglected boy. What had she done to find it? Precisely nothing. When she learned she couldn't rent a boat, when her fear got the better of her that first trip on the water with Barri, she let the plan slide, while continuing to imagine the deed whenever some jolt of Roger arose to snap her out of her languor. Now it seems the credit is to be Henry's, this perverse and wanton child.

You'd better show me.

In silence they leave the dock and climb the path. Still early, not yet time for the rest of the world to begin its weary waking. They continue in silence along the edge of South Baptiste Road to the place where Henry had stepped from the verge in his sleepwalk. At his silent direction, they turn left onto a small path that descends through aspen wood. They are through the wood, passing a rotten-timbered boat, almost to lakeside when she turns and retches into the sedges. White moths released from a tin box, is what Henry sees. He watches them go. He might have to pull Ydessa toward the lake. Yesterday he almost puked himself, seeing the black arm rolling in the water. How had he known what it was? He knew.

He sits down on a large flat stone and takes out his pen. I'm sitting over here when you're ready, Ydessa. He picks up an aspen leaf, still verdant, and on it draws a filigree of white moths released in flight. He stuffs the leaf into his pocket. A light rain is falling softly, making the green bower dance. Later he will copy the draw-ing into the book of speculations kept hidden in his room. He can feel a slight change in the charge of the lake. He wishes the charge would brighten her. He will not pull her to the spot. Perhaps the rain is encouragement for her.

She wipes her mouth and eyes in two quick gestures then turns and makes her way.

Show me, Henry.

He rises from the stone and moves toward the lake.

The arm is directly in front of him, rolling in the shallows. He points, his heart roaring. Ydessa peers down.

More than anyone should ever be asked to bear.

The arm is almost unrecognizable, the hand too blunt, but Roger's wedding band still shines on the pallid, bloated finger. She looks without comprehending, her mind breaking apart, scattered images break up into leaping colour. The husky she had come to adore, sitting tall, awaiting her command. A barred owl that rushes into flight. A crystal bowl, three rosy Macintosh apples.

Henry is seated on another flat stone, his eyes turned away. He roots through a square half metre of rotting material, making a pile of small shells, nuts, insect casings. He can hear her gasping loudly through thick strands of snot that run from her nose, her face streaming.

I can't face this.

Yes.

I mean I can't touch it. I need to retrieve it. I need Roger's ring. I need to go back to the cottage. I want Barri.

Okay.

You stay here. Or better yet, come up to the road and sit there. I'll go get Barri.

He doesn't argue. Don't cross her, he thinks. He would do anything she wanted. Anything.

As Ydessa and Barri walk toward him, he can see that Ydessa has a drink in her hand. Melancholy overtakes him. When Barri asks him to show her the way, he nods like a dumb animal and gestures to the path to the lake.

Take me there, you say to Henry. Ydessa can't. She's in shock.

You take hold of his hand and he leads you down the path to the water's edge. Points again.

That's not pretty, you say.

But you know what to do.

You can hear Ydessa's terrible sobbing on the road.

Ydessa wraps Roger's arm in a silk scarf, lays it in a shallow grave. You and the boy stand witness at grave's edge. You had to sever Roger's finger to release the wedding band. The ring is too large for Ydessa, but she carries it now on a black ribbon around her neck. She asked you to wrap the finger for her, and she places it in the grave next to the scarf. Henry replaces the soil as directed. Over the small mound of earth Ydessa sets a bouquet of cosmos and purple basil. She steps back, quiet as a stone.

The light over the lake glows lavender.

You read:

All goes onward and outward, nothing collapses,
And to die is different from what anyone supposed, and luckier.

It was an accident, plain and simple. You two are sitting inside the cottage, the sun dipping low in the western sky.

He left me, yes, Ydessa slurs. Plane. And simple.

You note the rage in her voice. She's been drinking steadily throughout the afternoon. You nod wearily. As in some second-rate drama, you see yourself making a scene, pouring the Scotch down the drain, an actor in this wretched play. In other dramas the drunk is slapped in the face, thrown in the shower, given hot coffee. You will do none of this. Too late. Not even a boat ride will draw her back to herself now. Besides, she can't be trusted to stand, not even on dry land.

He climbed into his Cessna as always, you tell her, well prepared for flight, thoroughly focused and engaged as always: think of this as a certainty.

Fastidious. Slurred, the word *hideous* swims to your ear.

Would you like me to make you something to eat? An omelette? Do you have eggs?

Ydessa's eyes roll in their sockets. She throws back the rest of her drink. Lucky I met you. She is leaning forward, the glass is heavy and sliding in her hand. It lands with a bang and a jump on the coffee table. I didn't know landlords like you existed. You are reallytrulygood. Starting to rise. She falls back clumsily into the sofa. Closes her eyes. I'll sleep. Sleep now.

And enters the sleep of ages, steeped in alcohol, ravaged, her bloodstream slowed. You watch her as she drops into the deep.

You lift her legs up from the floor, roll her gently onto her side, facing the room. You retrieve a wool blanket from the cedar chest and settle it around her. The powerful mothball scent elicits no response. You will stay with her.

Good night, Sweetheart. Sleep tight.

ELEVEN

SHE HAS BEEN many weeks away from Toronto. She has studied the wildflowers, learned a few of their names. Viper's bugloss, wild carrot, pearly everlasting, butter-and-eggs, bullhead lily, bird's-foot trefoil. Touch-me-not. Fleabane. New York aster. Forget-me-not. She's been reading books Barri placed in the cottage. God is dead and the deadness of God is the mischief of science, because science decrees we have gone successfully up the road a ways without Him and can go on this way indefinitely. But hasn't God circled round under cover of the new millennium to fall back into silence, alive but unsought? Silence isn't death, she is learning, though many think that to live in a sought-out silence is wrong-headed. She has observed how wildflowers will grow in cracks, how seed doesn't stay seed in stone. She has observed mysteries.

What is she doing at the lake? What has happened to the golden girl?

She told Barri that the first time Roger met her parents, Rose settled him on her chintz-covered loveseat then turned to the happy hour cart, asking, What is it your parents do? She gave him Canadian Club on the rocks then took up her own glass. *Prost.*

She raised her glass, waiting for his answer, not sipping until he spoke.

My mother teaches piano. My father disappeared about ten years ago.

Disappeared? She lowered her glass. You have received no words from him?

We don't know where he is.

But this is terrible. Why do you sit there so calmly saying disappeared?

We looked for a long time, but we didn't find him. He has truly disappeared.

Pish. America has CIA. Canada has what it has. These detectives can find anything.

Not always.

The mafia then.

Roger laughed. We have looked, my mother more than me. At first she looked furiously, tirelessly.

Oy. All her dreams must be nightmares.

I dare say.

Such a heaviness she must feel on her heart. And Ydessa to have no New York father. Sam will be everything for you two. Sam must be king of your castle.

Roger laughed. Why do you say castle?

O mein Schatz. Because you are such the dirty rascal.

A morning in early September. Teresa calls on Ydessa at the cottage by the lake.

This is a surprise. What brings you here?

I thought we might have a talk.

What about?

Your future.

My future? What's to discuss? In a few more weeks I'll go back to Toronto, if I can get my lazy ass in gear. The lawyer will tell me how to manage my life. Maybe I'll take up real estate again, reclaim my golden status, be hated by colleagues, attend concerts alone. My parents will drive me crazy.

May I come in?

Why so formal? Yes, come in. I'm going to have a drink. Want one?

No.

A towel hangs over the mirror above the sideboard. Ydessa pours herself a generous Scotch. Teresa moves to the old chair by the window and sits down. That's one way to start the day, she says.

Ydessa snorts. Did you come over here to insult me?

No. I'm worried about you.

I'm fine.

Teresa waits for Ydessa to say more, but there is no more.

Henry told me that in Toronto you live in a place called the rat race.

Ydessa laughs, takes a long draft. We all make out the best we can. What about you? You instruct bodies on how to stretch in space. People think you're operating a cult.

The September heat is rising. A motor starts up far out on the water. The day's patterns begin to open.

Teresa smiles. Yes, I've made the townspeople nervous, it's true. In the early days I received hate mail from Anonymous. But I've been of service to some of the women. You offer houses to the rich, I offer breath to women who might otherwise suffocate.

Come off it. People can't live on breath alone. We all need four walls and a door that locks. Everyone wants that.

You have walls and a door, but you don't want them.

Ydessa frowns. Really, such a jerk you're being!

Tell me.

I don't have to explain anything. A hole in my life. Things vanished through it. The heart is volatile, but it doesn't have anything to do with the condo, for fuck's sake. The condo is great.

She looks around, lifting her arms as if to grab something and wring its neck. It's not me who's cut off from her *wellness*. Get real.

Teresa clears her throat. Have you been thinking about leaving? We have to talk about Henry. He's become completely attached to you.

Henry is a child who wants a mother replacement, is all. He knows very little about attachment. He's quite special, but in some ways he's very normal. He wants someone who will never *ever* leave. I'll wager that he forgets me after I've been gone two weeks.

Teresa frowns. I must be seeing you in your past. It's taking a lot of time for your light to reach me.

What's that supposed to mean? I don't need a guru, Teresa, I really don't.

How about some dispassionate consultation? Could you use some of that?

I am a woman recently widowed, uncertain about what to do next. But soon enough time will heal me. How's that?

Okay. I get it. But what *are* you going to do? I mean, what do you want to do? Did you truly mean to stay here all these weeks, learning something about an unfamiliar place, simply to turn around and resume your old habits? Seems like a wasted opportunity to me.

The thing is, though, it's my fucking life to waste, not yours. Seeing me in a moment of weakness doesn't give you the right to advise me. You haven't a fucking idea about the complications of my life.

What I know about complexity might surprise you.

Look, I'm afraid this conversation is over, Teresa. I'm not the most confused woman that ever lived. I've not been squandering my time here. More like biding my time. And yoga. What about yoga?

But are you waiting for something to happen?

Ydessa looks into her empty glass. That, my dear, is a very perplexing question.

———

A storm is upon them, racing from the east. Wilson has crawled under the bed. Three-kilometre thunder, crashing and rolling, lightning cracking. Ydessa's mind has shrilled. She lifts her eyes to the window but sees nothing beyond her own reflection, a second self in a bed of tousled linens dressed in expensive lingerie. Sky obliterated.

The storm moves nearer.

Passes overhead.

Gone, behind which a milky pewter light — pale green with pink trim, above and below clouds that still run wild.

You and Teresa sit at the picnic table in twilight, the air full of song-bird *chet* and *peep*. You are taking note of the many exquisite turnings as day becomes night. Fresh peaches and tomatoes combined in a salad of leeks from the small garden between tall pines. A loon has been calling to its mate in its highest register, a frantic plea: *Are you there?* Now the calling has ceased. Daylight inches away, water darkening below the evening star that now steps forward.

At the heart of each of us is another, a beloved, coming home. You do not wish to talk. You are listening to the lake.

A light, swift and brief, appears in the cottage window, the outline of a shadow jettisoned, distinct, expansive: a quasar. Then the light goes out. The skin across your forehead tightens, the weight of your mood shifts. You wait, motionless, tensing in the dark, posture of acute expectancy.

Teresa has been talking awhile without an audience. She laughs. People who have not yet mastered their past, people with situations more complex than ours. More nuanced. Did I ever mention how hard I find most people to take?

A pomegranate is set on newspaper on the table, a gift. A

meteor falls, swiftly, in the eastern sky above Teresa's head, a real beauty that rushes away, leaving behind a sorrow impossible to trace.

Distraught in the little white cottage, Ydessa has pledged to end her drinking, refuse all company until sobriety kicks in. She's completely unfit for anything except a little housework. Maybe tomorrow. She rises from the bed, goes to the bathroom, turns on the light, removes the towel hung over the mirror. Inside the mirror her childhood bower springs up, a shelter made beneath the overhanging boughs of a spruce tree, far removed from the house and her mother's activities. She can hear her father, come outside to look for her. *Come and join the party!* Her mother sits by the swimming pool, laughing with friends, making rounds of wisecracks and practical jokes. She has served doughy white bread sprinkled with sugar, cut into shining stars. They wear silly hats, drink bright cocktails in dark glasses. Banana splits are served. Sinatra sings, *Fly me to the moon*, her mother is in mules with pink feathers. Some of the feathers drift tenderly across the surface of the pool.

Through rooms painted in eggshell and sky blue, beyond the front door and out into the neighbourhood and its clean streets, her father goes searching.

Ydessala!

She turns out the light, goes back to bed.

She dreams of her adolescent self, a fly encased in amber, preserved by Rose. Suspended animation. Her friend is allowed to come to the house, can stay for dinner, can sleep overnight in her bed. Together they are permitted to pore over her books, to make fun of preposterous social propositions. What she is not allowed to do is run in the streets. The manners she is allowed are those displayed on 1960s TV shows. Beneath the boughs of the backyard trees, she dreams a perfect and meaningful adult existence, while Rose suppresses memories of millions of people in troubles grave and wide.

In the morning she drives to Bancroft to use the pay phone.

Marc says, You park yourself for weeks in a nice cottage on a lake, you read books, you take yoga classes. Meanwhile houses listed with you are going to competitors. Come back next week, or nevermore. I mean it, Ydessa. This is your last chance.

Well then, if you mean it. Thanks for everything. Goodbye.

She lowers the receiver. What does she need to think about work for? She is, as her lawyer has said, a wealthy woman.

She stops to buy groceries at the IGA — apples and eggs, coffee and biscuits. The essentials. In the parking lot she falls on the black asphalt — nothing there to trip over — groceries flung wide. Her mother, a quick and shining fragment of memory, dances past her, singing. *The world wants your light.* Her left knee is bleeding. She lies there for longer than she knows is reasonable. A man in a breezy Indian shirt finally helps her to her feet.

She has rifled through cottage closets and the medicine cabinet but cannot remember a first aid kit, though she thinks it unimaginable that Barri would have overlooked one. She limps back into the store: rubbing alcohol to clean the wound, some gauze and tape to dress it. Scissors.

In the centre aisle, unseeing before tins of coffee, Henry is weeping, small fists pressed into his eyes. His shoelaces have come undone and are lying loose on the floor. His clothes are filthy as ever, his hair matted. A woman, in evident disgust, pushes her shopping cart in the widest possible arc around him.

Henry.

She extends her hand, stops. Places it lightly on his small shoulder. Henry.

The room inside him where voices gather is rampant with commotion, crowded and full of yelling. He tastes fire. Strange cacophony of wordless voices, noise fanned with black wings. Standing alone — or so he feels — while his father is making up his mind, far gone into his bees, and Ydessa is leaving, her departure imminent. The fact of these two losses — father to bees, Ydessa to where he does not know — cannot be borne. He stands in otherworldly communication, which he doesn't understand and can only receive in profound agitation.

What is it, Henry?

He turns to her, removing his fists from the bowls of his eyes and crying out. My father is taking me away.

What? When?

Very soon.

If only she believed in the mysteries, if only she believed in her ability to receive the mysteries, she might be able to acknowledge the space around him, which has turned a brilliant ultramarine, the blue of a flaming gas ring. Instead, flooded by anxiety, she kneels, flinches, the contact bringing her back to her purpose. To get away from the suffering. Her head is bowed. She ties his shoelaces.

My father is in aisle two. Henry's eyes have rolled round. He is examining Ydessa now. I know where they keep the bandages. Fifth aisle. He takes her hand and leads her.

In the frozen food section Henry's father is counting bills in his wallet. When he sees his son passing at the top of the aisle, he shouts loudly. Henry! Where's the tin of coffee I told you to get?

I'll get it, Papa, and he runs off, leaving Ydessa to face the father alone. He is so much younger than Ydessa had imagined, mid-twenties at most, only five or so years younger than she is. His face carries little emotion, but something flares below its surface.

You the woman renting the Grew place? Long holiday you're having.

Like Henry, his eyes are startling blue, his hair long and tousled. She feels the silence ballooning between them but can't help looking: he is beautiful. Otherworldly. So beautiful, anyone could easily be caught up, studying this face, with Henry deep inside the man's features; the son, roaming unpredictably, might leap out at any moment. The father shakes his hair away from his face. He is waiting for her to speak. She takes a wide step back, remembering the sapphire on her finger. Puts her hands in her pockets.

Henry says you keep bees?

He meets her gaze. I did keep them, till recently, when wasps grabbed the queen. And the workers killed her replacement. So no hive now.

I had no idea wasps kill bees. I thought they were the same creature, more or less.

He frowns. Time to give it up, I suppose. I'm the kind of bee-keeper that knows almost nothing about bees.

Henry draws up alongside his father, a large tin of coffee in his small hands. Here, Papa.

Good. How much?

One hundred and ninety cents.

Okay. I'll get your tinned tomatoes.

Okay if I drive Henry home? Ydessa asks.

The father turns to study her. If Henry wants. You want to go with this lady?

Henry nods.

Be home for dinner. He leaves them, pushes his cart to the other end of the aisle and disappears without another word.

They fly like a pair of birds along South Baptiste Road in Ydessa's convertible. Ydessa steers away from Henry, keeps a distance. Separation and cohesion, equally balanced.

My dad doesn't know too much about you.

No.

But he let me come with you.

Yes, he did. That was trusting.

Can we go visit Barri?

Yes, let's do that. I'll take you home after a short visit with Barri.

You can take me home so my dad doesn't worry.

Right.

He continues. I went over to the lodge. I visited the mother cat. Have you gone over to hold the kitten?

Ydessa bears down slightly on the gas.

At the cottage they first head toward the water to entreat Wilson from his usual hiding place. So he won't be jealous, Henry said. Sitting carefully in one of the wooden chairs is Alicia Campsall, Roger's mother, dressed in an expensive linen suit.

You have never been thinner nor more attractive, she says,

seeing Ydessa.

A small Louis Vuitton suitcase is positioned neatly, midway up the path to the cottage.

Ydessa turns.

Henry, go on over to Barri's. I'll be there in a minute.

He stalls, begins to speak, but she shoos him with her hand, and quickly he turns and runs up the slope to Barri's door.

Ydessa turns back to Alicia. If I'm different it's because I'm tenderized by grief.

For god's sake.

It's not been easy.

Who says it has? Listen, I've come to take you back to New York with me. What are you doing here, sequestered in this desolate place?

Desolate? Look around.

Sam and Rose didn't work hard to raise you so that you could loll in this dull and uninspiring place. Roger didn't marry you for you to hide here. You are, like it or not, a Campsall now You're breaking your parents' hearts, all alone here.

I haven't been alone.

Stop. Alicia raises her hand. I know all about grief when it's feeling sorry for yourself. You can come mourn with me in New York, like a good girl.

Am I not allowed to mourn in my own way?

Don't be ridiculous. Making a complete mess of things. Your parents beside themselves, calling me every other day, asking me, Is she maybe insane? You're not the only one in the world who has lost someone. Many wish to comfort you, why deny them?

So this is about receiving comfort from Rose? What nonsense. And Sam? He's got enough on his plate. I find it comforting here. I have made friends here.

Ridiculous.

In the heat of early September, with gauzy light dazzling the surface of the lake and an unseen hawk crying above the treetops, standing before her stylish New York mother-in-law — designer suit, expensive luggage — Ydessa's mind begins to close around the accident, around what she is doing, what she has done. Months, years: a failure.

Her bloodied knee pulses. How did you get here?

Alicia smiles. What do you think, honey? I'm a New Yorker. I ordered a car.

What if she were to place herself in Alicia's hands? Would she regain some old assurance that life was real, not a fluctuating spectre commandeered by strange geometries? Pack up the car, drive back to Toronto, fly to New York: why not?

I must go up and see to this bloody knee and that little boy, whose name is Henry. But first let me get you settled in the cottage. You'll take the bedroom. I'll sleep on the couch.

No. I'm not here to disrupt everything but only to remind you that I exist, that your parents exist. I am your *life*. Did the thought to call me on occasion never enter your head?

Alicia lifts her suitcase. Ydessa wrenches it from her hand. Why did you not call *me*?

Alicia is mumbling behind her, watching her feet as they climb to the cottage. This is not about your life only. This is about family. He was my son, the son I bore.

In the kitchen Alicia reaches into her purse for her cigarettes, opens the pack, lights one, inhales deeply. Ydessa goes to the bathroom to clean and dress her wound. When she returns Alicia is sitting by the windows. She takes a chair opposite. Henry will have to wait.

From where she sits she can see Daisy chewing on an old bone, back legs splayed, neck and tongue at work to plunder the bone for marrow. Moored to the dock, Barri's father's old mahogany boat rocks gently, moaning low as it rubs against the pilings. A motor far out on the lake synchronizes sound, wave, and wind into something Ydessa had come to notice and find peaceful.

How far away is that peace now.

You have always approached your difficulties sideways and on the run. Why would Roger's accident change that, I suppose.

I am not on the run. I am stopped. Stymied.

Alicia pulls herself up in her chair.

Who lost Roger? I lost him. Rose and Sam are grieving for the loss of him. *Stymied.* Please. There are obligations to fulfill. I have come all this way to return you, not only to your people but to your moral obligations. These lake people are not your business. Really, taking yoga classes, while at home your mother weeps for how she has failed to raise a daughter who knows better than to boycott her love, a mother's love. It is shameful. Perverse. You know the right thing to do, and you do not do it. Come, now, shake yourself loose from whatever it is that holds you to this perversity.

This is bullshit.

These are not your *people.* This is not your life. Come back to your people now. Come back and mourn within the circle of our love. Are you getting all this?

Oh yes.

Good.

I'm getting how you couldn't attend Roger's funeral, but you've made the effort to find me now. The only reason you've come here is to interrupt the humiliation you say you feel. You're such a snob.

You're horrible!

Ydessa stands and crosses her thin arms over her breasts. Circle of love, that's a laugh. Circle of mirrors is more like it, everyone making the supreme effort to position themselves so that only they are reflected, and in the best light. I'm getting how I will not give my life over, not to you, or Rose, or Sam, not to anyone. I could go to New York with you. But don't imagine that my reasons would be your reasons. This is my life. *My* life.

Nonsense. Utter nonsense. Of course Rose and Sam have no idea how to rein you in. Survivors often don't. They do their best, but to help you take a next step is beyond them. In the long run, if you meet your obligations, you'll be glad I came.

Weeping openly now, Ydessa turns away. You blow my mind, Alicia. There is not one convention I would follow to please you.

Now *that* is truly amusing. You've been a conventional girl your whole life.

T W E L V E

YDESSA WAKES IN dim light and lies quiet. After a few minutes she turns on the lamp. Henry is standing at her bedroom door.

My god, the stealth of you, she whispers. You got past Alicia without waking her?

Henry nods. If you show me how, he whispers, leaning over her, his breath warm in her ear, I'll make you a cup of coffee.

We mustn't wake Alicia. We were up very late.

Henry nods.

Ydessa lifts her blankets, looks in, rolls her eyes at Henry — completely naked. He leaves the room. She rises to put on the same dress she's worn for the past two days, an emerald green linen shift, light and pleasing, brought by Alicia from New York. She goes to the bathroom, fumbling in Alicia's cosmetics bag for aspirin. No. She tiptoes past Alicia. Asleep beneath an eiderdown in the living room, she has flung one arm out from beneath the cover. The pearly light coming from the bedroom shines dimly on fine skin, white and dry, like the wing of a moth.

Henry stands at the sink, coffee pot washed and inverted on a paper towel.

Show me how to make it the way you like it.

They stand together, waiting for the coffee, arms about each other's waist. She can feel excitement in Henry's small body, its heat and ease. He watches, enraptured, enjoying the coffee's smokey aroma. She retrieves her cup from the drainer, removes a second cup from a cupboard, motioning silently, You too? You'll try a cup of coffee?

He nods.

They stand at the counter, sipping from their cups, as sunlight enters. Henry makes faces after each sip.

Don't keep drinking it if you don't like it. Everyone knows best where his own shoe pinches.

He shrugs.

Let's go see if Barri's up yet. Boat ride?

His eyes blaze.

C'mon. She lifts the coffee pot from the burner and motions toward the door. Shhh.

At Barri's mudroom door they stop to watch her at the kitchen sink where she is washing dishes, bathed in morning's attenuated light. Ydessa knocks softly.

Children! Barri moves to the door, smiling. Come in.

We're here for our morning boat ride. Ydessa raises the coffee pot. Henry made coffee.

Did he.

Yes. He had a cup. Thinks it's awful.

It is awful. That's what sugar's for. The thermos is there on the counter. I'll get dressed.

Had she really been comforted by her stay at the lake, as she'd said? It seems to her, setting off from the dock, that she might have exaggerated the quality of her months with Henry and Barri, not quite as glorious as she'd wanted Alicia to think. Ydessa and Alicia had talked late both nights, and while they talked, her resolve had leaked away.

Had she even once let down her guard, spoken plainly to Barri about her life with Roger? Had she cried out for help that terrible day, accepted the proffered small plot in Barri's garden, yet never confided in her? Her reticence had likely been obvious from the day Barri first set eyes on her. She has the charged pose of someone who is one step away from retreat, and now, in addition, she must abide her mother-in-law's rule. This juggling she will find tiresome.

In her seat in the boat, Ydessa fidgets, her eyes darting from shoreline to hill. Finally they come to rest on Henry, who sits opposite in the back seat, drawing her portrait in profile. A headache pounds. Her mouth is exceptionally dry. Everything is too bright, too loud. She twists the sapphire ring, handling it nervously. She will be a good subject for Henry, she thinks with a half smile, he who likes best the lively, the energetic.

She should give back the ring. Impulsively she removes it from her finger, and turns in her seat, interrupting the child at his work, her voice soft below the motor's din so that only he can hear.

I can't keep your ring, Henry. I've worn it with pleasure, but you must save it for the woman who'll be your love. Take it back now.

She thrusts it into his small hand, but he doesn't receive it. He rears back, pushes her hand away just as she releases the ring. It flies up over the gunwale and falls into the lake.

No. Oh my god. You can't!

Henry, feeling within him the arc of the ring as it flies, has flung his notebook aside and thrown himself, wailing, onto the thwart. Rings of water press slowly outward from the spot where the ring has silently entered the lake.

———

You hear the commotion and kill the motor.

You turn to them. What's happened? What's wrong?

The ring! Ydessa yells. It's fallen into the water.

Sweet Jesus.

You start up the motor and circle back while Ydessa keeps shouting There! There! pointing to a miserable empty pocket of blue water within ever-widening circles. Henry's cries echo across the land.

It's pointless, you think as you turn the boat around and around, pointless and heartless and pitiful. O but why should this have happened? Roger's wedding ring, you assume, once more descending inexorably through the water, to join the detritus on the bottom of the lake, to lie there for eons. It's pointless. At this spot the lake is thirty feet deep.

What'll we do? Ydessa cries.

We'll go back to shore and take Henry home. There is nothing more to be done.

You imagine the scene that may unfold: Henry as he enters his house, undetected by his father in the kitchen, Henry as he goes to his bedroom and closes the door, climbs onto his bed and lies there, face down, cheek pressed into the pillow, mouth open, tears thick, legs and arms limp, his body expanding. As if what happens to Ydessa happens to him too.

After docking, after lifting Henry from the boat, after placing him in the car with Ydessa's help and driving him home, after watching him drag his stricken carcass across the yard without turning, as he usually does, to wave, you sit with Ydessa, who runs her shaking hands again and again through her short hair while you observe her from the driver's seat, helpless.

THIRTEEN

IN THE DREAM, his mother — standing behind his father as his father gathers, then cups to his open and unprotected hands, a small mudra of bees, winding them into a kind of comb, one hand wrapping strands of honey around their tiny bodies until they are encased in a honey cocoon, their bodies startlingly yellow, bright, buzzing, the sound enormous. And Henry — standing on a wooden chair with his small hand held aloft, drawing the shifting grid of currents as the bees buzz, tracing in intricate detail the perfect geometries of father, gilded bee, and field.

His mother smiles.

Henry walks the secret path from the road to the lake, through dense wood, past little mounds of insect casings and fir needles. The sky is fluid, working its blue light into his thoughts. He sees

Joe Baptiste cross the lakefront in his bark canoe, reflected in a mirror that captures Henry's own twin. Ancestor, Aboriginal man who loved this beautiful lake, who did not call it names. Friend, not foe. Who fished its waters, trapped along its shores.

He will not hate the lake for its invisible hand. What fell has fallen. When the water caught the sapphire and drew it deep into itself, his mother was drawn then too, weightless, dazzling, down into everlasting.

But a terrible cry travels up his throat and escapes. Startled, a brown thrasher rises up out of the edge of the wood and begins at once to sing the song of ages.

He sits in his now-filthy new jeans, cross-legged on the ground, making small mounds in the dirt from gathered moss and stone and leaf. For two days he has waited at the back of the cottage for Ydessa to appear: an agony of waiting. She doesn't appear. Alicia doesn't appear. On this, the third morning, you bring pieces of buttered toast on two porcelain plates, and together you wait, eating in silence, the breeze warm, comforting. Henry traces with a crust patterns made by the melted butter on the plate. Some butter falls to his lap as he lifts the crust to his mouth. You wonder if you'll ever keep this kid clean.

Did you find out whether the lodge still has kittens?

He nods.

What say we go over and pick one.

His head shoots up. Who for?

You smile. Me.

On the road to the lodge you take his small hand warily in

yours, your mind lit, the terrible emotion you feel flooding you. To keep your equanimity you scan your body for sensation.

Henry is looking through the trees to the lake.

This one's all we got left, the cabin girl whispers, pulling a wicker basket from beneath a low step. This here's the runt. The kitten has been sleeping in the hiding place. You stand aside, watching Henry tease it awake. It comes up out of sleep with a tiny trill. He smiles, drawing the kitten to his chest and holding it carefully there. He kisses its tiny head.

He turns to you. What will you call her?

I'd like it if you would name her.

He smooths the fur on the tiny orange head with long, delicate movements of one finger. He presses his fingertip against the fine white fur beneath her open mouth. Together you observe the kitten's cool gaze.

Bird.

Bird, you think. *Strange.* Okay.

After a while the mother cat appears and hunkers down in the shade of the steps.

That's the mother. Could we take her too? Could we keep them both at your house?

Oh. You had not anticipated two. Two was not the idea. Are two as easy as one? You have no idea. Poor Daisy. Half-baffled, you study the mother. The tabby returns your gaze, briefly, the contact undeniable, like a trickle of water to an unrealized thirst.

And what's her name to be?

Blue.

Said without a moment's hesitation. *Bird. Blue.* All right. Let's go to the desk and make our arrangements.

Henry looks as though he might burst.

You take Henry with you to the shops in Bancroft, looking for a used travel carrier to transport Blue and her kitten home. Why must we buy a used carrier? he wants to know.

You tell him it is pointless for people to continue to buy new things when plenty of used things do a job adequately. But he has never heard of shops that carry used things other than clothes.

Where will we go?

We'll try a thrift shop called Choices.

There are a lot of smells in here, Henry says, as you wander up and down the aisles.

People's clothes sometimes carry smells.

Like B.O.?

Well, the shop won't likely try to resell clothes that smell bad. Put your nose to your own skin. What does it smell like?

He lowers his face to his forearm. After a while he says, Nice cookies.

I've always liked older styles, you say. You pull a cowboy shirt from a rack. See this? Probably from the 1950s. Probably hand-made. I've bought most of my clothes second-hand. Cast-offs, some folk call them. But they are often better made than new clothes.

My dad says only poor people wear second-hand clothes.

You stop to look at him more carefully. If you'd had a younger brother, maybe your dad would think differently. Those kind of second-hand clothes can be godsends. Hand-me-downs, they're called.

You're using a lot of old words, he tells you.

Words you've never heard before.

Yes.

Well, words come and go.

You find a carrier at a Goodwill shop, made of wicker, its handle in poor condition. We can fix that, you tell him.

How?

Would you like me to show you how?

You know so many things, Barri. You're like Merlyn. Those old clothes at Choices are like time moving backwards, aren't they? He stops to consider what he's saying.

Sometimes Ydessa thinks too fast, he says at last.

In the Bancroft liquor store the absence of pink rosé is irrefutable evidence of how rural peoples everywhere are unhinged. Everyone in the city is drinking it, Alicia had said. I mean absolutely everyone. Rosé had to be downgraded to a Verdicchio, a doubtful one at that. Downgraded too were hopes for foie gras and Kasseri cheese. How do these people live? Alicia asked, overtaken by pique in aisle two of the IGA, where she made the sudden decision to have the party catered.

And so it was: a catered party, no matter that the guests, including Alicia, numbered only five, no matter that one was a despondent nine-year-old boy. Having been told of a local young woman who was making a small fortune with gourmet sensibility and business savvy, Alicia called from the pay phone. She ordered Grilled Chicken with Lemon and Olives, Potatoes Fontecchio, Figs with Crème Fraîche and Raspberry and Sherry-Vinegar Purée. The figs will have to be ordered from a specialty shop in Kingston, the young entrepreneur told her.

Yes. Fine. Of course they had to be ordered, but they *could* be ordered, that was the point, sweet and plump figs, perfect food for a goodbye. If you would be so good as to arrive by five on Friday, we will be ready to receive you. We will expect the chicken to be not quite piping hot.

At four o'clock, Teresa called: something had come up, something she had to attend to, she was terribly disappointed, and of course would be there but for this unavoidable conflict.

You probed. Is everything all right? Henry will be inconsolable.

Oh, Henry. Yes. I'm sorry. You will have to offer diversions. Reading? Drawing on large paper? Bring out your paints, a little time together, just the two of you in the house?

Yes. Good idea.

Through your front window you watch the dockside preparations. Alicia unwraps fine crystal wine glasses from tissue paper. A woman who could not be dissuaded by even the sanest rationale. Why would Ydessa go with her to New York, unless to avoid conflict? Nothing for Ydessa in New York.

A fine damask cloth billows out from Alicia's raised arms and settles over the table. On the cloth, in a cut crystal vase, she sets an extravagant bouquet of what look to be wild asters, forget-me-nots, and pearly everlasting, mixed with cultured roses. Where have the

INSTRUCTOR

crystal, damask, vase, and roses come from? Only the dishes are yours. Grew family heirloom, white on white, circa 1910, strictly for renters' use now, given to you by your father after your mother's death. You watch Alicia's movements with interest, see how it is she means to impress you, is eager to impress you. She has not understood that you can't be impressed by high society, having spent your young life watching your mother perform in these ways.

Henry has arrived. He stands with his back to Alicia, vigilant, silent, watching the cottage in anticipation of Ydessa. When Alicia pauses to talk to him, you can see that he does not answer, but looks away, retrieves the pen and sketchbook from his pocket, holds them like a shield.

The boy has arrived, Alicia announces. He's down on the dock without shoes, and he's sour. You're going away too, I reminded him. Princeton, is it?

Picton.

New school, new friends. You'll be busy, I told him. You won't even remember Baptiste Lake.

What did he say?

Nothing. Mute. A stone.

Stone? No. Not a stone. A minor falling star, a boy capsized, was more like it. Ydessa cannot face him yet. She goes to the living room and takes up again a book of short stories she had chosen haphazardly from the cottage shelves, searching the pages for a word she might borrow to give their reunion purpose. Graceless. The story makes her jumpy with its forceful verbs: shoot, snipe, swipe, careen, burst. They depress her, these quick verbs. She sees

127

how deceptive her love of speed has been.

She must go down to the water, must deal with Henry, must allow the burgeoning tension to overwhelm her, the loss of the ring amplified on this first meeting since then. And she must observe without reaction how her mind closes like a fist around the jump inside her, must observe what is so energetically lifting within her — her own terrible effort to denounce the love that binds the boy to her. She must go down. She is fond of him. Okay, she loves him. But his mother's ring has been carelessly lost, and to add to her sins she has to tell him that she'll be leaving soon, that the decision to go to New York with Alicia has been made, made by her alone, a decision she came to in an enormity of shame.

Henry looks at his feet the minute she arrives on the dock, not once does he raise his eyes to hers during the meal. She sits, attended to by servers charged with duties ranging from serving to cleanup. For these two women, who hover inside the cottage while the meal is consumed, Barri has set up coffee, biscuits, a cribbage board. In bright September sunlight, Barri makes a silent vow to receive everything Alicia needs to give, to eat slowly and carefully, praise every effort made, in a manner of delight generously and openly expressed. Alicia will be allowed to catch and hold Barri's gaze as often as she likes. Conspiratorial, she will think.

On this afternoon Ydessa drinks seven glasses of cold wine. She sinks deeply into her cups, plays with her food, slouches in her chair, casts about now and again in utterances so incoherent that she is, finally, ignored by all except Henry, who bears every word.

The sky is a bowl breaking into flame, the world is drowning in tangerine light. You sit back in your chair. A rare event, Alicia. No other renter has brought such luxury to the cottage, and I thank you for it. In July — was it? — my friend Teresa arrived with a picnic basket full of surprises, and we ate on the dock. It was a little like this, minus the figs, Verdicchio, and damask. Henry had his first fresh tomato sandwich that day.

Ydessa nods, eyes closed.

You've been very kind to Ydessa. I want to show my appreciation.

Using the blade of his knife, Henry redesigns the remains of purée on his plate, the knife point clicking against the china. His left hand lies tense on the tablecloth. Alicia puts her hand over it.

Henry removes his hand.

The lake is slate-grey, seersucker.

You lean forward to stroke Henry's cheek. I've been thinking that you must take Bird with you to Picton. My mother used to say a kitten can be a trust to hold. Your father would likely agree, if I asked him. I'll have to keep the mother, though. Your father wouldn't agree to two cats.

Henry receives the news without looking up.

Ydessa opens her eyes to take in his response. Nothing.

Henry. She is rising unsteadily from the table. I have been a drinking person all afternoon — and I'm sorry about that — but you and I should take a walk.

No.

Yes.

You should not take a walk, Alicia says.

It is then, at last, that Henry's eyes meet Ydessa's. He pushes back from the table and rises to take her hand. They leave the dock, climb to the top of the path.

They walk the road in silence while all around them the woods release their autumn sounds and scents. As they round the bend at the small causeway, Henry spots the evening star and makes a wish. Soon he will be standing before her for the last time. Soon, but not tonight. Tonight he must be with her.

My son was capable of lasting friendships, unlike his father, and, if you will permit me, unlike Ydessa, who is impossible. Roger knew Ydessa very well, just as she is: beautiful and humourless. Stiff. Caustic. He was always telling little jokes, sly self-deprecating ironies, encouraging her to lighten up. Quite out of the question, as I'm sure you've observed. She's a perfectionist. She always needs to demolish opposition, wham! Roger was absolutely the best boy. When he was a teenager he adored the cinema, all those glamorous and moody actresses of the thirties: Bette Davis, Katherine Hepburn. Do you know the film *Christopher Strong*? He must have seen that film ten times when it played in repertory. Did you see it?

You shake your head.

Hepburn plays a successful and rather daring woman, a pilot who flies around the world. Women such as her, unencumbered by strong feelings of duty to the feminine, enraged Roger's father, but Roger, defending her, would say, No, she's perfect.

My father encouraged me to wear trousers.

Your father must have been a very progressive man.

He was a family physician, a good one, capable of thinking in umpteen shades. He was also an activist. He believed that wasted resources demoralize a community, and that resource degradation expresses an underlying hostility. There were uranium mines in this area, and my father fought hard before he died to limit contaminant released after the mines were decommissioned. Tons of radioactive tailings were left to dry out above ground during a policy limbo. Unmanaged tailings become like fine sand, you see. They infiltrate and contaminate both air and water. Uranium binds to soil, so crops and bees, our own health, are concerns here.

Are you a physician also?

Me? No. My father's daughter, is all.

Surely you have a lake association, a lake plan? The people of the lake, by which I mean, people like yourself, local people, people who live here. You will have concerns about these dreadful cottagers and their more dreadful nostalgia.

Dreadful? Nostalgia? You laugh. If you were to stay awhile you would discover that the lake is thick with meaning for everyone, whether short-term or permanent.

Oh I'm not staying. No, Ydessa and I will soon be on our way. Nothing for the likes of us here.

You smile. With all due respect, I've always thought one's place is wherever we say it is, the place we treat with affectionate regard. In any case, Baptiste *has* been Ydessa's place.

In a book taken from the cottage shelves, she reads about a novelist who becomes famous almost overnight. Men and women send him letters in which they claim kinship with him, shared destiny. In one letter the writer includes her photograph, and tells the novelist she is fated to be his lover. Briefly a flame flickers, brief recollection of a letter she composed, but never sent, to a marvellous stage actor known to be unassailably gay. The memory is sudden and revealing, catches her like an electric shock.

The night before Roger left for his fishing trip, side by side on their backs in the dark, he had confessed his old fear that he was unlovable. But I think if someone like you can love me, he said, I must be something.

Little fishes in the lakebed, little ponies feeding, obedient to the first cause: hunger. What sort of fish? Lake trout. A child descends a ladder to the lake floor, crayfish and worms in his hand. Sediment stirred in a dart of minnows. Anchorwoman sends out a breath, a wave. Another loss. These lack persuasion. She adds volume. Stirred in the sediment field, a coffin hinge. A bone. Stardust.

In the morning Henry walks to the big house. A dead mourning dove lies by the side of the road. He'll stop to give it a proper burial. Is someone shouting? How early is it?

Henry slips past you and heads to the basket where he knows to find Bird. He lifts the kitten to his chest, kissing tenderly her nose, her eyes. The mother, awake on the sofa, raises her head.

I love you too, Blue.

TWO ‖ AUTUMN

O N E

WHAT I WANT you to think about is moisturizing. Accessorizing. Roger's mother smiles.

Ydessa sits with Alicia in the first-floor living room, Alicia's cairn terrier on her lap. Just now they are having coffee, served in Alicia's fine bone china. The dog is attempting to bite Ydessa's nose.

Accessories are not in the forefront of my mind, she says, while pushing the dog away.

Alicia raises an eyebrow but says nothing more on the subject. Did you know that cow bone ash is the material used in bone china? No, I didn't think so. Hold your cup up to the light. You see its warm colour, its translucence? You won't become a vegetarian who refuses to eat off bone china, will you, obsessed by yogic ideals? Those people are tiresome.

The little dog jumps down from Ydessa's lap, sniffs the air, draws back his ears, winds himself round then drops to his belly on the carpet, hips splayed, chin on his front paws. His eyebrows twitch furiously. Ydessa watches him watching Alicia: two women and a little dog, silent among the appurtenances of a richly appointed room. They sit in lush sunlight, a beautiful September New York afternoon, with cumulus clouds drifting above the penthouse.

In all his beautiful courtesy, Roger enters the tableau. An abstraction. Ydessa senses him at once. He cranes toward her. She holds her left hand up so he can see that she's wearing his too-large wedding band on her left hand, secured on her finger by the diamond he gave her. He smiles. Nods. *Accessories*, she mouths. She looks toward the window, where oscillating light begins to trumpet a thousand memories. *There is a bird.* Like a bird, abstraction flits from woman to dog to woman to man, trailing patterns as of red thread. By its affectionate hold on the mind the four are linked.

A young and tender shoot of a woman about to be run down by a crashing, earth-moving mother-in-law: explain that to a bright nine-year-old boy.

Now she belongs to the sisterhood of widowhood, a female sub-group, a sorority she had never imagined. She is travelling in unanticipated directions that reveal something new and ugly about her life. Such useless activity. Rage. Relief. The newly widowed, offered the chance to alter her life, defends herself against what is indefensible, with self-immolation, with an unaccustomed lunge at purity of belonging to this world and none other, this world an agitation of imagined rooms behind mysterious doors. She is failing miserably.

Henry! Ydessa put down her cup and took him in her arms. He was choking on his tears.

Alicia leapt from the couch. My god, what an inhuman cry. Help the poor child.

I'm trying!

Give him an apple.

An apple?

For god's sake. Alicia grabbed a red apple from a bowl on the table and shoved it at Henry. Eat this, child, she ordered. Bite!

Henry did as he was told, and did not choke. He bit into the apple and held the piece in his mouth until the memory of how one ate returned, and he could chew. He chewed, swallowed. The choking ceased and his tears subsided. His face was pale. Ydessa placed her hand on his thin shoulder. Alicia stepped away from their little scene and left the room.

Ydessa took the apple from Henry's hand and led him to the old rocking chair. She sat him down in it, took the chair opposite, and waited. After a while he spoke.

I'm going to have to go to a school in Picton. My dad says it's better to be on your own and free than stuck in a noisy prison cell, multiplying and dividing. But I have to go to school in Picton, because it's the law there.

It's the law everywhere.

Henry considered this. He asked, Will you make observations in New York?

Observations?

The tall buildings —

Skyscrapers —

Yes, the skyscrapers. You could observe those.

Observe.

You won't think about me, not exactly.

Not think of you?

No, you'll be watching patterns. Like I do. You'll be thinking, Beauty first.

Beauty first.

Yes. That's it.

He leaned back in the chair and crossed his ankles. He kept his eyes on her.

You could sit in a park.

Central Park?

It doesn't matter. Any park. Observe the birds and the trees and the ground as the birds pass overhead.

I could watch their shadows sailing along the grass.

Well, that's just an example. It doesn't have to be birds, or trees. It doesn't have to be shadows. You could watch people. People make patterns too.

He took hold of his elbows. He nodded encouragement at her and she smiled back at him.

Alicia entered the living room, dressed in her linen suit, hair combed and pinned up, her wonderful perfume filling the air.

Are you all right now, Henry?

Yes.

Well, it's time to say your goodbye to Ydessa. We have to pack up the car and be on our way. You're sure you're all right? she asked again.

Yes. Thank you for the apple, Alicia.

That's quite all right.

He untangled his limbs and stood up. He took Ydessa's hand, holding it very lightly.

Ydessa—, he began, but she stopped him.

I'm sick with shame about how I lost your mother's ring, and I'm sorry. You may doubt it now, but I love you. Never forget that I love you. Never forget our — what we did together at the lake. Now you'd better go. *Go.*

He did as he was told, flying out of the cottage, running up the path to the road. Startled a small rabbit in the long grasses. It stiffened, hunkered down, leapt away.

Voices thick upon him.

After a downpour the night streets are glistening, twenty kinds of light reflected in rainwater pooling here and there along the sidewalks, twenty enticements in as many directions along the avenue. She walks at random, in and out of circles of bright light, passing people crouched in doorways, their tiny theatres neon-lit. The city's grid is competing energies that collapse into two elements: light and sound. She studies the neon, a muffled sting of buzz in the wet street. First observe beauty, Henry said, but the longer she observed the neon, the less she saw. Open. O.P.E.N. On East Sixty-Second Street, the signs are not only at street level, but also above it. Observing, opening to neon's buzzing vibrations, tilting her head in homage to Henry, she experiences a hollowing, crushing hunger in her solar plexus.

Neon. Abundant in the universe, rare on earth, a collective retinue of other liquids and gases, mercury vapour, for example. Will observation alone reveal all there is to learn about the matter of the world? No.

Later, in the New York Public Library, she reads about neon. Later still she begins to learn that what drifts upward through the observed, what drives upward through the geometry of the observed, is not cold, derelict, menacing fact, but rather haunting and fleeting traceries. The counter-impulse to attentive looking is panic.

Every square metre of the sun's surface is constantly sending out energy equal to the power of seven hundred automobiles. About one two-billionths of this energy reaches us in the form of sunlight.

Sunlight is a mixture of colours. Auroras occur from about one hundred to one thousand kilometres up in the air. At these heights, so little air remains that space is almost empty, like a vacuum or the inside of a neon light. The shifting glow of an aurora is essentially electrical and somewhat similar to the light from the neon signs along any Main Street.

Observe.

But her mind is too quick, too much in a hurry. Swamps easily. The night street glistens pink then green, twinkling, delicate, dangerous. There is too much street, too little Ydessa. At times she longs to press down through asphalt, push her body through and arrive on the street's underside, static and cleansed, aerated by small particles, to look from below the street while millions tread their horizontal lines, orderly and trackable.

She keeps to the side streets, trying hard to avoid the refuge of the bottle. New York, New York. O.P.E.N. everywhere. Eat me, drink me: the city a system of need and supply in hues of indigo and violet.

Henry had learned about bees by studying their patterns. But he learned about some patterns by reading books his father gave him. He read about the correlation between the height at which bees will build their hives in summer and the amount of snow that falls the following winter. He preferred not to speak to his father about this, not to reveal what he was learning, nor to question astonishing facts, but about this one he asked, How does winter know the height of summer hives?

His father's tone was heavy with warning. You ask too many questions, son. You keep asking questions like that, you're going to see craziness in this lifetime.

His father had been right about school. Henry was a prisoner serving a sentence teachers forced him to endure. Nights, he walked the fields, or read his books, or played with Bird. In these ways he restored what school tried to drain out of him: curiosity, a pronounced desire to go and go and go into the quick of thinking, going thick and alive.

The school librarian was the only adult willing to enter his life. She prepared a list of books for him to borrow and supplemented his curiosity with good cheer until a sudden relocation ended her days at his school. He missed everything: Baptiste Lake, with its curves and stones, enticing drives and narrow paths that led nowhere and everywhere. Barri. Teresa. Ydessa. Blue. He had never been fearful at the lake, never afraid to prowl. But Picton seemed full of unknown forces that crept and dodged and slid and hid and pounced. He walked the back streets timidly, hands thrust deep in his pockets, had anyone cared to notice.

He studiously avoided the drinking teenagers and the old men who met on the banks of the creek. Learning the difference between sharks and dolphins had been at first futile. So many dolphins turned out to be sharks, there seemed no way to tell which was which. At school a boy stole his pen and taunted him with it, holding it just out of reach, daring him to climb onto the back of his chair and lunge after it, which he did, tumbled, and scraped his arm along the linoleum floor.

Henry Rattle, we will distinguish ourselves from the animals, if you please. Give him back his pen, Rufus.

The dilapidated farmhouse Henry and his father now lived in, out beyond the fairgrounds and the Crystal Palace dance hall, was a kilometre from the school. In order to avoid the creek, he headed into the broad fields south of the farm, drawn to the apple orchards and tiny ponds, fields of alfalfa and waving corn. Combines on the move there, cyclists on the road, who sometimes raised their hands to wave, and he would wave back, tentatively, missing Ydessa keenly then. Light on the corn was golden on those first evenings, the gold in small part assuaged the longing, which roaming in fields could not mitigate. His bones slowed. He carried a strange languor beneath his skin, was confused by an unfamiliar feeling of ennui.

His drawings changed.

How to sketch colour, he wondered, how to catch light as it streamed down in columns, how to mark paper with the lines of colour made by the setting sun, by the disappearance of sunlight? He would hold his capped pen aloft and draw in air until the light turned violet, then indigo, until cornflowers alone lent the world its colour and light. His own suffering was a pattern that tormented him. He could not draw it, could not get it down, not even with the pastels he began to use. The magical evening light, flickering, flowing, was a balm that would not soothe. On his first evenings in the county without Ydessa, on the dark side of evening's veil, he ran home to Bird as if pursued.

She entered a bar, took a stool at the zinc-topped counter, and ordered a double whisky, which she drank quickly. Another, please.

The octagonal stone of Henry's mother's ring had been set high in platinum. In this New York autumn, on this New York night, the sapphire rose in her memory, free of its deep burrow in sand at the bottom of the lake, to pierce her. She sat in uproar, fighting things of air.

TWO

TERESA ASKS, IF you were to learn from your partner on your deathbed that he had been having an affair with your best friend, could you resist the desire to dwell on this betrayal above everything else? Could you remain focused on your own life?

How cruel! The woman lying next to her shouts as they receive their IV drips in the outpatient clinic. Thinking only of himself, the little bastard! She shakes her head.

It's the best some people can do.

Not good enough. Not by a long shot.

But do you think you could keep from getting triggered? Teresa persists.

The sorrow of loving such a man, is all the woman will say.

The sandwich treatment: chemotherapy, radiation, followed by another bout of chemo. Then a two-week break from treatment, followed by a new set of tests, and another prognosis.

You wait for Teresa on a bench outside the hospital. As she comes through the revolving door, you stand, your arms opened wide.

Here I am, all chemicalized, she says, falling into your embrace.

Braveheart.

In the car on the drive home, Teresa reclines, talking with eyes closed.

I might say to such a man, My death will be your tragedy, buddy. I'd want to say it matter-of-factly. What a poor fucked-up shit. Looking for reassurance from a dying woman.

After a while she continues. It's hard to stop my mind from clenching in the old ways.

She presses farther back into the seat. Likely this nausea will continue all night. I thought I had lost my nerve, but guess what, I never had nerve.

The drive is marked by brief silences.

My misapprehended life: all along it was scruffy and odd, not amounting to much. I wish I'd said to that woman, His life belongs to him. No matter how angry we are at men for how they bludgeon us, the simple fact is — o this head of mine — what is the simple fact?

It's hard to be singular, alone with the decisions of your life.

Is that it? Sweet Jesus.

I'm afraid so.

Teresa smiles. I devoted my life to teaching and am therefore on very familiar terms with the part of me that wants to be marvellous. There I was, wanting to be marvellous for that woman in the clinic. If on my deathbed my partner decided to tell me he'd been having an affair, I can see myself trying to illuminate his situation for him. You know why?

You think, Stay quiet, drive her to safety. You can do only so much.

What I would be thinking is: manipulate him by being marvellous. Make him indebted so he'll give me what I want.

Which would be to end the affair?

Oh, that's delicious. Is that what you think? No. What difference would it make then? No, here it is: quit being a child, looking for attention and approval. Keep all that shit to yourself. Don't involve me. That's what I want. She smiles weakly. But hey, in other news, tell me again: what's that sticking to my skull?

Thrush feathers, chestnut burrs, thorns of cabbage rose, worms that suck your brain, moss, gall, sepals. Protective armour.

Teresa laughs. Bloody hell!

Your life belongs to you, you say.

I never wanted to raise a man. I didn't want to raise women either. Is teaching the same as raising?

She goes quiet. After a while she asks, How long since either of us had a lover? Must be ten years for me. You?

Maybe twenty.

Teresa opens her eyes briefly to observe the road. She crosses her arms over her chest. Coughs a little. I guess the truth is I couldn't tolerate the short shout in bed followed by those long, terrible silences.

After a while her breath becomes soft, her head drops forward, her knees fall open.

You adjust the heat.

Beneath the heavy wool beret, she is bald. Her eyelashes are gone and most of her eyebrows. She wages her battle with the Taxol, exhausted, brought to bone in relentless search for a narrowed and sharpened mind. But mind is fog.

She is skin and bones, you think, blood, yes, and breath.

She sleeps.

On the porch of the studio, yellow birch leaves swirl and scatter, illuminated by the overhead porch light. A light breeze catches the edge of a piece of paper tacked to the door; it lifts and falls.

Yoga Classes Cancelled Until Further Notice.

Practice nonviolence, truth, non-thieving, sexual continence, and non-covetousness.

A young woman stands at the door, reading the note. She looks at her watch. She cranes her neck, looking into the twilit sky. Leaves chatter in the treetops. She lifts up onto the balls of her feet and extends her arms slowly to the trees, hangs from the lower curve of the waning silver moon like a marionette. Drops arms and slowly turns away, speaking softly to herself.

What day is it?

It's today.

Oh. My favourite day.

While New York's morning engines roar in the streets below, Ydessa rereads Barri's note a third time, weeping furiously. The gross injustice of cancer, come to someone like Teresa who practiced stillness and deep listening for hours every day.

And then suddenly there it is, that bird of vision, the slight arrival not quite itself, that has made such effort to stay concealed. *Everything changes.*

Ydessa takes a sip of her drink. In the next room a guest with some talent is thundering on Alicia's grand piano. She has to strain to hear what Keith is saying.

Alicia calls you the golden girl of Toronto real estate. I suppose she thinks New York will bring you round. But who would want it? You know that buy-and-sell world is a joke. If I were you, I'd be taking daylong sojourns in the rooftop garden on a chaise longue, watching the clouds sail by. Disassociate from all thought. Pray that your mind drops out. That you might break out of a fundamentally flawed way of thinking.

Heat in her temples flares, panic rises. Keith raises his hand to console her but stops short of touching her.

So much can *happen*, Ydessa. My lover, Daniel, died in June. Another AIDS tragedy, unmourned by the world. I brought his ashes home, and as I placed the urn on the dresser, I thought I heard a voice cry out for help.

What?

I cried for days.

She looks away, takes another sip of Scotch. "In the Still of the Night" thunders out on the piano.

He laughs, a high note. In response to the mystical, Golden Girl goes mute.

She listens for a moment to the buzz of the penthouse, many

guests by now intoxicated.

No lover really leaves. Someone you've made love to many times? No. I talk to Daniel night and day. He's always with me.

You think he called out to you? That his spirit came to you? What can I tell you? Just — wait. Be open, is all I'm saying.

I'm restless. Quick. One foot out the door mostly. And very cynical.

Alicia's guests are in full flight. The rooms crackle. Sweet aromas drift as the caterer and her young protegé bring around canapés and drinks. The protegé brings Ydessa a large glass of Bunnahabhain and now offers Keith more wine.

You'll want to let go of your anger soon, for your own sake. You'll want to step back from it and observe how, when anger starts to boil the blood, it makes the mind yell out infantile complaints. We are highly compulsive creatures. When you become negative, watch how often complaint follows on the heels. Not. No. Nothing. Never. Negative words. You've got to note the negatives to discover your next move. Set the intention to build a better vocabulary. Empty your mind. Move slower and slower in your mind, let go of the negatives. Finally you'll just stop.

They are standing at the window, looking out over the city. The lights of New York twinkle below them.

See that? He points to the south. Rockefeller Center is private property. Security trolls move around the halls looking for incriminating evidence, because nothing and no one is safe in America. Those guys think they're seismographs, capable of measuring the future. They make a good living reducing all kinds of complex questions to simple propositions. Those guys are in the halls of private skyscrapers all over Manhattan. What I do, though, is I slink about in the subway paths, security man for HIV. How to really measure ignorance? I wonder. That's how the whole thing got started. I saw those guys go up into the air, whereas I go down into the earth, an earthworm down in the tunnels, pushing myself beneath the city. I use thick lines when I draw. Arteries wide open. That's how I keep things going. I'm a security man, a gay security man.

Let's go up to the roof.

Is it safe?

Safe? Have you been listening to me? Come on, you can tell me all about your young genius.

They sit side by side in lounge chairs beneath a clear sky.

They call it sky management. Everyone seems to agree there should be some kind of law against light trespass in New York, but no law has yet been passed. New Yorkers will never have the good fortune to see three thousand stars, like you could in the country. The New York sky is a grey lid.

She tells him she was afraid of the dark at first. Nights at the lake, she made her way slowly, creeping from the cottage down to the dock, the sky with its myriad constellations never noticed before. At first she'd race back up the path, suffering from vertigo and nausea.

Henry — my little shadow — coaxed me into slowed down observation. He taught me things like. . . that's Cassiopeia hanging upside down and undignified over there.

Did he really talk like that?

Yes, he did. It was so surprising, given that he was unschooled, and practically an orphan, for the little interest his father took in him. But clearly his mother had talked to him. Barri talked to him straight across, nothing patronizing. She spent time with him.

And you spent time with him.

I don't think I gave him one thing, and yet he clung to me.

Oh fuck. Just stop it. I can't stand self-deprecation, mine or anyone's. I'm twenty-eight years old, a fag confronted by a plague. You're what? Thirty? Married three years to a guy who died unexpectedly, brutally. This is life: fall and recover. Why should anyone ever want us? We're unstable. We don't recover. You and I should get our shit together. We should go prowling together in places that give us the heebie-jeebies.

All I've ever known are the heebie-jeebies.

Jesus. How you're golden beats me.

No, this is really true. I never used to walk in the streets. I was always in my car, always on the run, between houses, between sales, queen of real estate going home at night to count her spoils. So many times, while buttering his toast, or riding an escalator, or sitting next to me in the car, Roger would say, Try to believe in *something*. He didn't know the half of my faithlessness.

Keith laughs. Sure he did. Our Roger was a man of scrutiny. But now, in any case, ladies and gentlemen, here comes the new Bloom. Here comes the sun, here comes the four thousand three hundred and sixth drink of a lifetime. Here come the things we do and do not do. The idea of permanence and perfection is a protection racket, Ydessa. *Try* to believe in something. Try to *believe* in something.

They are laughing, holding their sides, cut loose, swooning with relief. She is drunk on his peculiarity and his trust by the time they bid one another good night.

THREE

IT IS SAID in Japan that one boy alone is one boy, two boys together is half a boy, three or more boys is no boy at all. Henry alone is one boy so gentle, so light-fed, so ragged and scruffy, so unformed but ingenious, the future speaks to him as he walks across the fields. What the future will deny him he does not know. As he walks toward the harbour, he hears distant laughter. Drawing nearer, he sees a wedding party, men in grey suits, women in milky green gowns, all sitting together by the water, the bride and groom drinking something in tall glasses.

It is Saturday, a day very often without reproach. Cumulus clouds are monumental above the bride's head, shocking white against the blue sky. Radiating joy unbound, the bride moves among her party of loosened souls.

Henry sits on the grass watching her, with everything on earth and in heaven preparing for unexpected leaping emotion, and now here it is.

Look, shouts one of the bridesmaids, there's Cinderella's coach in the clouds. She's comin' round the mountain, she's drivin' six white horses.

Silver laughter. The bride turns to coax a kiss from the groom. Applause.

Henry watches the sky, happy, as the foaming white horses and billowing coach slowly dismantle and slowly reassemble into a towering anvil, advancing thunderhead. A parade of cool shadows follows. The wedding party rises reluctantly from their chairs on the grass and heads indoors.

Henry rises.

Along Main Street, among the Saturday shoppers, he can hear snippets of conversation, townspeople complaining: blue day gone, storm coming, too many rainy weekends, where's a decent climate, you find it, I'll go there. Walking among the lamentation, he feels bruised. He smells the rain. He won't seek cover.

He tries to imagine what Ydessa might be doing at five o'clock on a late September Saturday in New York. He can't. His eyes fall to the sidewalk. The question propels him forward, away from the harbour toward the junction. Businesses fall away, the broad fields loom.

Someone has dropped a shoe, it lies lost in the grass. Henry picks it up and holds it to his ear as he has seen others do with a ribbed shell.

Hello? You dropped your shoe.

A rolling rumble of thunder shakes the earth.

A black cat, thin tail held high, is picking its way delicately among the short stalks of harvested corn as Henry walks slowly along the edge of the road, reading its progress as if that were his own tail swaying there. More rumbling. The black cat bolts.

Bird will be hunkered down beneath his bed.

Under the weight of heavy black cloud he stumbles. He knows the rising wind says it's time to seek shelter, but he doesn't want to. To be out in the open, observing and measuring the wind by the speed of the storm in its terrible power: if he stands, already electrified, until fully inside the storm, he might feel its great heart pass right through him.

A blaze of lightning strikes the billowing sails of sky. He holds his pen up to the dark clouds to gauge their speed.

He shouts, and high wind kicks the sound behind him. The skies open and rain pelts down. He holds his pen high, tip pointed. He shouts again. Lightning splits the clouds. He plants his feet more firmly against the gale, now rocking him, the grasses battered flat then switched up as if maddened awake, howling wind and grass and horizon a sea into which he is swept, small blasted Odysseus. The hard rain crashes down upon him. Wind swamps him. Still he holds his pen high against the heart of the storm, crying out to the spirits writhing and leaping in tumult. The massive cloud splits, like high waves heaving against the tumblehome of some heaven-bound ship, the sections part, one side, the other, as the vessel presses on through hammering thunder. Lightning forks into the broad fields to his left, the grasses undulate like surf, thunder pounds and reverberates across the land.

He stands firm, his pen held high, his voice raised, howling.

FOUR

TERESA STANDS IN front of the bathroom mirror, surveying the wreckage of her skull. She tucks one thin rope of hair behind her ear and holds it there with a child's plastic barrette. The barrette falls away and hangs, swaying.

Your time hasn't come. This is illness. You are out of balance, you don't know why. You need to come back into balance.

She turns from the mirror.

Don't play that game with me. You and I both know what the problem has always been: cigarettes. I professed to respect life, did so most convincingly while I puffed away on the cancer sticks. That's what they're called — cancer sticks.

You don't know. Etiologists don't know. No one has said unequivocally that cigarette smoking causes cancer. Every illness is made up of so many unique variables that it's impossible to know. You couldn't forestall what was meant to come even if you did know. To stop a thing is not always possible.

She snorts.

You think illness a confession of guilt by the body. Try not to grow imaginary fifth limbs and a second head so that solid earth might be restored.

I acquiesce to my dying, Barri. You won't change my mind.

Teresa sits on the bed, swings her legs off the floor, lies back against the pillows and closes her eyes. You must examine your attitude toward reality.

You stand next to the bed looking over her. I must?

You must, because this is my death, not yours.

You drag a chair bedside and lean in toward Teresa, who, in her small torment, eyes closed, says, I'm so sick of words.

Beyond the house, in the tall pines, a raven calls, a call you love. Imagine the deep purple lustre of its feathers. Its voice fades, the wind settling.

The room settling.

Chelsea Piers is a place of shades of grey, derelict and filthy, but you and I will improve it, Keith tells her. They walk slowly, arms linked. I had this idea of becoming a good artist. I wanted to get my hands on large canvases. I wanted to paint the Guernica of the 1980s. So I thought. I pursued this idea.

Ydessa is pale, silent.

After Jonathan's death, Roger and I had no appetite, not for flying, not for painting. It was as if desire had been devoured, gone out of the world. Roger went to Toronto and I went to the Lower East Side every day, alone, to eat Italian cakes and drink espresso in family-run cafés. I watched the mamas and the papas with their children. I watched the carnival, Italians and Jews and hip radicals and the mean and hungry poor. In the evenings I went to bars. On the TVs there were shows like *Miami Vice* and *Three's Company*. Surreal. In the days after his death, with that notion of myself as a painter sickening and fading, me a charlatan, with genuine street life coming awake every morning — the poor, the immigrants, the artists — all shouting, all colourful, in the mornings and in the evenings, the surreal cold and hyper light coming from those TV screens — the situation was strange, I was a stranger in my own city. I remembered our laughter at Jonathan's bedside, the sheer exuberance, and ever so slowly I resumed the old, energetic urge that wanted thick lines on murky subway walls. Those drawings seemed to me to come from a place of exceptionally dark beauty. Someone called them offensive.

His thinking swerves and suddenly fails. She notes his uncertainty, words coming more slowly. He turns to catch her response — then loses interest.

Say something more, she beseeches. Anything. A platitude, an old lie.

But he doesn't want to speak.

Say something.

Everything is so trite.

Her legs begin to buckle, she begins to falter, leans over, retches. She drops to her knees on the sidewalk, palms pressed against the asphalt.

Ydessa!

He kneels next to her, placing a hand on her upper back, the other on her forehead.

You're burning up, sweetheart. I've got to get you home. Can you sit over here on the stoop? No taxi's gonna come along this street. I've got to go over to Tenth. You stay here. I'll get us a car. Can you stay here?

I'm cold.

He drapes his leather jacket around her shoulders.

It's not great here, a bit creepy. Meat-packing district. Not glamorous. Look, mostly just fags going out to the clubs, but if anyone tries to talk to you, tell them to fuck right off.

This is a small and repetitive movement, a repetition become familiar in its go-and-go-around, containing an image of Roger calling to her in the urban dusk. Here alone, anguishing in this incommensurable place, she strives after an old intimacy, he calls out to her, I'm here, and she calls back, Don't leave me.

Alone, lost, irrelevant, all at once — squarely facing the eloquence of a mortified body. No chance of resolving the repetition — she's drifting toward the rapids now. One and the same, one and the same, dancing and draining in the glorified dark.

She shivers there on the stoop, half in love with the ongoing, unresolved tension. Then a pair of dark, ragged shoes stop before her.

You alone?

She looks up.

Not smart, out here alone.

No, not smart. I'm waiting for my friend.

Give me some money.

I don't have any money. My friend has all the money. He's coming.

The man leans toward her. She can smell alcohol, sweat.

What's wrong with you, girl?

I'm sick.

You all bones, that's for fucking sure. You got no meat on them bones. He is whispering, placing hands on her hips then on her pubis, pressing hard, lifting a hand to her throat.

Ydessa closes her eyes.

Now you're ignoring me. That is just like a woman. For that you got to pay.

He spits a bullet of phlegm in her face.

He brings his fist down hard on her pubis.

Pay!

He tightens his hold on her throat. He moves his hand between her thighs, pushes two fingers into her vagina.

How's that slit, you cunt that don't wear no panties.

Stop.

Don't see you putting up much of a fight, rich girl like you, sitting out here alone, being sick and all. Not wise to ignore me.

The begging in her voice. *Leave.*

He pushes his fingers hard into her, thrusting twice before removing his dirty hand.

You got to pay, cunt. I'll take those pretty diamonds you're wearing. Gimme those rings.

He pulls her diamond and Roger's wedding band from her finger.

Nothing personal, bitch.

And he runs.

Keith arrives in a taxi, gathers her up, strokes her hair, guides her into the back seat of the cab where she lies down, her body furled, undone. He gets in next to her, places her head on his lap.

Lexington and Sixty-Seventh, he tells the cabbie.

F I V E

AGAINST HER WILL she surfaces to find herself half out of a dream, looking around dazedly at partially remembered things: a certain fall of light, Teresa in Adho Mukha Svanasana, holding yet not holding the position at the front of the studio, arms straight, eyes closed, feet bare, legs relaxed, like a figure cut from wind, with her Tibetan bell close at hand.

To address the dream, to say, Teresa! Only then will she open her eyes. But you speak while lying in corpse pose only if you have something urgent to say. She wants to say not one, but every urgent thing. About life, death. Roger.

No, she can say nothing — not to Teresa, not to a living soul. Before words are even uttered, concessions have to be made. To give up immediately, as soon as thought forms words. The notion recedes. She becomes sullen, withdrawn. For how can she express what so achingly presses against her heart? To want Teresa's knowledge and help and have no chance of it, here in this city. To want now what she has made so little use of — how it angers her, how it sets her entire body upon the pain, the awful wrath of the heart.

O! She calls out to Henry's mother's ring in the benthic zone of that faraway lake, calls out to chastise it for leaving, then coming back again and again *and again*. Her memories of Roger seem to abate, then he reaches out his arm and stops her. Barri and Henry — they reach out.

The penthouse dissolves into a primal loathing out of which a hand surfaces, and on its fingers rings, blazing, blazing, accusing. Every direction blocked, every idea repudiated, every flimsy prop revealed. She is no one at last: here in New York City, nobody, alone, before an impasse that will not yield.

Where to go now, to what place, to seek what she lacks? She is not lost, no. The thing she's been sick for, for as long as she can remember, was never missed till Henry drew its image.

She is standing in the penthouse kitchen, scouring a small pot where scalded milk has stuck. The milk resists her efforts, and a small voice says, It's all right, you've got enough, no one will notice or care.

She is walking alone in brightest daylight on Fifth Avenue. Ahead of her, two women draped in mink and ermine stroll arm in arm. She reads their gestures, traces of fury in her roused heart. She remembers Barri and Teresa.

The small voice mutters, Live and let live.

She sits on the lowest step of a staircase in the Grand Central concourse, stupefied. High south-facing windows admit the sun, which pours ropey shafts of thick light on the marble floor. Men and women in heavy wool coats are standing together in groups of three and five, spotlit by the falling light. She is on this marble staircase in Grand Central just two weeks before Christmas, surrounded by glitter and fairy dust. She has been with Alicia for three months, staying in the immodest penthouse on the Upper East Side. Right now she is absorbed by this slow swing of thick light across an animated world. Remembering Henry, she recalls his adage: Beauty first. She sits, observing the faces around her. Horrid: laughing, grimacing, their imagined small talk tedious, hideous. How to get close to her life?

Henry lies on his belly, swinging a paper mouse back and forth across the floor, attempting to entice Bird, who crouches beneath the bed, pupils expanding and contracting like small tunnels as she watches, readying for the pounce. Made of Christmas wrapping paper, accordion-folded and dangled from a piece of red ribbon, the mouse skates across the floor. Bird studies the sliding enticement, its trail and arc, its energy. It gathers, spins, releases, spins, and releases once more.

Henry can hear his father folding newspapers in the front room. A silent, narrowed man. Outside, the snow comes down thick and wet. The drifts accumulate, a slow white herd, tableau after shifting tableau, forming and reforming across the frozen fields. The snow will make for bad driving conditions, loaded cars on the country roads travelling between houses, to and from Christmas dinners. Not Henry. He'll be at home with nothing very special to eat, just a chicken and some cake brought to the house by a thoughtful neighbour.

The kitten catches the mouse, disembowels it. Now the room is renewed, quiet and still after the ruckus of wrapping paper. The books he studies tell him that nothing is ever still.

He turns over on his back and lies gazing at a depiction of the solar system that his father has pinned to the ceiling. The galaxy within which this solar system rides is made up of billions of stars, this galaxy one of a cluster of a thousand galaxies, one of thousands of such clusters, a galaxy for everyone who lives. Our sun is a star, out on the rim of the Milky Way, a pea on the edge of a very large plate. Our entire galaxy is spinning such that it would take our sun about two hundred million years to go around. The limits of the universe are not known. This fact Henry dwells upon dizzyingly.

We are small turbines of heat revolving in unknowable space, unknowable and limitless.

He reaches down and draws Bird and her tattered mouse up onto the bed. He remembers a conversation with Ydessa.

You're a strange one, Henry. Up very early, outside immediately to observe the birds waking and the flowers opening.

Chicory stays open till noon.

You see? Who else knows that? Who else gets up early so as to be right there when the chicory opens?

I don't know. What do you do in the mornings?

I pace. I pace in my dreams and I pace when I get up. I pace in front of the kettle set on the old stove. I hug my arms and count the number of seconds till the water boils. I put a paper filter in the coffee cone, I measure out enough coffee for two strong cups. Pacing. I wonder about the great blue heron. I notice the old kettle rapping as its metal heats and shifts. I ask myself what I am doing at Baptiste Lake. Fidget, flit, pace, and pounce. That's me. Flit and fidget, whereas you sit quiet. Still. Deeply patient. Observing the fluctuations of the world, as you've said: chicory on the move, a quarter inch an hour, the arc of the sun, or the crowning of a cumulus cloud.

You're going, whereas I look around. You're quick. I'm slow.

Quick? Impetuous is more like it.

You think you're doing something wrong.

Well, aren't I? Going around in circles all day? Never accomplishing anything, never achieving anything?

Achieving?

You want to get things done in a life, Henry.

You do things. You pace. You hug yourself. You imagine the great blue heron.

Ack. What are these things? Worthless selfish activities. I used to flip three houses in a week.

Henry laughs.

What?

Flip a house.

It's an expression. But the point is, I used to be inside that life, doing these things. Now my life is just a salt doll in the ocean, as my Poppa says.

Salt doll because of your husband?

Ydessa has covered her eyes with her palms and is making a washing motion.

Is it? Is it because of Roger's death? I don't know. Am I just supposed to spin and spin?

Is there someone you could ask?

She takes her hands from her eyes.

Well. That's funny. Someone I could ask. I'm kind of asking you. What do you think?

He had not known what to say. An answer? No, he didn't have an answer. Only his own observations, his curious drawings carefully stowed away in a book. Her yearning for answers had filled him with something like a flashing signal, hard and bright. He wanted to pass this signal back to her, to give her something to preserve and safeguard her no matter where each of them might go, no matter the distance between them. She was flamboyant, seeking, arms opened wide, tanned and thin and beseeching, brown against a wide blue sky, with the August pines throwing out their pungent perfume. Tell me what to do, her arms said.

He lies on his back, the centre of his chest lit. Bird nestles in the crook of his arm, her ears twitching furiously. Her fur is soft, her purr loud. He pets her while gazing at Venus, its elliptic bright and steady near the centre of the map. Many times he has drawn the colours of Venus, evening star, morning star, steady above the horizon in violet skies. In September, in a kind of agony in his new house, missing Ydessa, his future plundered, his father gone to try once more with bees, lost to Henry except sometimes meeting him over his questions and shining, trying to encourage him with a slow, distant smile, even while his posture spoke defeat. In September Henry lay in the grasses in the broad fields at sunrise and made his wish upon the lovely Venus. Let Ydessa find her sun path. Give her colours she can use. His palm held the memory of the ring he had once clutched in his pocket, like twinkling laughter, like the joy he had tried to bestow.

The snow descends outside the window, flakes glitter in light cast out from the room into the quiet night. He watches one flake after another as it falls, petting Bird. A slight draft in the room. He shivers. Bird's ears twitch, her eyes become steady. Each snowflake has its own aura in shades of purple and blue. The night is alive. A small boy's heart grows cold.

In the room inside Henry where that pure hard signal for Ydessa had blazed, voices are sounding, low and moaning, like wind in a chimney, deep and streaming, mud-soaked, thrumming. In the chill of the heart, in that innermost room, ancient voices rise, clamouring, a wild cacophony. Henry stirs. He lifts the kitten to his chest and holds her there, rocked by her purring, crying softly as he strokes her head.

Tears come thick as milk. He squirms — his mother is in the room.

Is she? He feels her hand on his forehead, but when he reaches to take hold of it, his own hand passes through air.

In you I suffer.

Mommy.

And in you your father suffers. You'll have to go with him to his beloved bees. Walk the line with him. You'll be all right. Where hundreds of bees gather. Walk with them. Walk through them. You'll walk unharmed, though your father's pace will feel so slow and grim. O my heart.

Mommy!

Do you catch what I'm saying?

It's too hard, much too hard. She needs to slow down. He can't understand.

The hive addresses itself not just to the eye but through the eye to the heart. You see? Study the country fields, the fierce December winds, the tattered heads of summer blooms, the jack-o'-lantern in the ditch that the neighbour has thrown to her cows for winter feed, the white stones in the old cemetery, how like brown apples descending, this snow that will not stop. This is the honey line. It will stop you for a drawing, you and that fountain pen of yours. With equal eye regard your father, the bees, and the droning earth that sings all around them.

Stop, Mommy.

Not the confrontation, but the integration. Who is the predator that tries to maim instinct? Who tries to steal fire? It has always been yours, to know the unseen helpers who hold you in the night. We are waiting to cross. Wait for me, she whispers, at the place where three roads meet.

The room shines bright, his small bedside lamp glows warm under the pink shade. Bird's tail flicks back and forth, her yellow eyes shining, her ears alert. Night descends. The room is charged, something electric set swimming in air. The old ones have stopped moaning. Their skeletal bodies clack. His heart is ice.

He lifts his head from the pillow, sits up, reaches for his note-book, and tries to record the fallen shards, the wreckage, the energies unleashed within the room. It is too hard, much too hard for him. He puts the notebook away and lifts Bird again to his chest.

He remembers the drowned rabbit Barri carried from the lake to the door of her mudroom. He thinks of Roger's severed arm, rocking gently in the foreshore. He thinks of the lake's August green, birchbark, and tall pines, how the trees flowed away from the lake, all in all, and also singular and distinct. How last summer was exactly enough, was just right. And then, just as Merlyn warned, did he lose his love? His body hurts as if it has been burned.

SIX

HER CANCER IS stage four terminal, she's been told to get her
things in order. And now, in the palliative ward, she will observe
from the higher mind, while below, in a scattered place, old harm
inflicts a fantasy that wounds her like a blade. A photograph on
the cover of a magazine catches her eye, a seashore image with
words written large in sand with a stick — *I miss you and I love
you*. She thinks of the man she once loved long ago.

She sits for an entire afternoon alone in her room, looking
out the window. She feels a simple gladness lifting within her as
she watches moving shadows cast by birds soaring high over the
hospital's sunlit trees and lawns.

Will it be reason or instinct, or a practice strengthened and
redeemed over years, or destiny, or alchemy, that pulls her mind
finally away from the fantasy? Hours drift by slowly. Barri arrives.
Teresa continues to gaze at shadows.

Then a sudden image arises in ferocious clarity: with one
swift strike she tears the head off the neck of this man who so
long ago forgot how to keep his love. A low, deep moan of grief
is in her voice as she turns to Barri and cries, O. My. God.

———

And so in the spring Ydessa returns briefly to Baptiste Lake, seeking the thing she lacks. The April roads are slick. Snow, lightly falling, mixes with icy drizzle. Nightfall. Ydessa turns in at the cottage drive, her fog lamps beaming over the darkened bare trees, over the cottage drive rutted and slick with mud. The tires catch in the muddy grooves, dig in, then stick, spinning.

Surely the ice on the lake will go out any day. You have assured her that the mergansers and loons will appear instantly thereafter, but the beauty of the seasons, coolly observed, won't be enough to keep her year-round, on the shores of Baptiste. This is not where she will remain.

Ydessa has not kept her resolve to move clean and sober into this next chapter of her life. She won't remember the drive from town tonight, drunk and high as a kite. A miracle. You arrive at the muddy scene to assist her, carrying a large flashlight. You can trace the lunacy of her attempt to steer the car out of the mud. You try to convince her to be carried up the path and into the house. Fuck off. She will make it on her own, she will take her time, and this taking of time strikes her as so funny, she has to sit down on a large stone and wait for the hysteria to pass. You get her to her feet, your arms around her sunken chest, knees astride the driftwood she has become. You lift her into your arms and struggle up the drive to the house, over the threshold to a kitchen chair, and set her down.

I'll make a fire, you tell her.

You fill a large glass with tepid water and set it on the table. You find a wool shawl your mother made and wrap Ydessa in it. You fetch kindling from the mudroom, return to the living room, twist newspaper into paper ties, and lay the fire.

You okay in there?

Yes, okay. Cold. I'll drink this water.

I can't hear you. Hold on.

Ydessa picks up the glass, takes a long draft. I'd like to see Henry.

The fire is about to take hold.

What? Henry?

Ydessa crosses her arms on the table, lays her head on her arms, *Henry*, and is instantly asleep.

You return to the kitchen, stand over her awhile, then remove her boots. You leave the room with the boots, return with a towel, bend to soak up the mud and melted snow. Though she seemed light as driftwood before, it's a strain for you to carry her now, the heat is tearing in your muscles as you bear her into the guest bedroom and lower her carefully to the bed. You leave the room, retrieve a blanket from the cedar chest, place it carefully over her. Turn out the light. The fire is roaring. A strong wind blows across the flue, singing as it passes. You sit at the window and study the fog rolling in lavender moonlight.

You walk along the shore in high waders, plants bowing before you then springing up behind you. The sedges are covered with goose feces, an accumulation worrisome for you and the other residents. Silt pollution is a worry, as is the need for restoration of wetlands and shoreline. These liminal places of earth and water lit by the sun, powered by the engine inside every green thing. You walk slowly around muskrat mounds, careful not to disturb nests of all kinds.

Birds' eggs are hidden in dried sedges and moss. Your listening is keen as you walk. Rainwater dropping from conifer needles etches the leaves below. Your listening gathers force. It plummets into more profound depths, penetrates mudflats. Blood that is slowed, that buzzes, air that noses an orchestra into sound, water that ceaselessly cascades through curving fractals, enclosures, the lake a mirror today, a place of infinite images, this morning's blue, small flying machine falling, filling blue. You are listening with such intensity you feel nauseous.

Assembling and limitless, Anchorwoman offers up a severed wing.

Ydessa rouses, startled, her hands thrashing away the thick smell of wood smoke that suffuses the atmosphere. To walk above the lake into the hills beyond had been her idea. Instead she fell into a desperate sleep, drunk in the grasses while fine snow fell and melted instantly, soaking her face and hands, cold seeping into her skin. Come over for a drink, the man in the bar had said. Come any time. I live on the far side. You can see my place from Barri's.

She shudders at the idea of seeing him again. Now the sky flushes with pearly light. He had approached her in town, boldly, not like a city man. In the city she could bring a certain advance down to the ground in a split second, without a word. Strangely she had agreed to go with him from the bar to a room at the Sword Inn, where Teresa would never be now, exchanging impersonal mercies throughout a cold afternoon.

Now night is falling. Her throat fills with disgust. Electrical currents whip in muscles that will not relax. Early May: the ground is cold and ugly. She must not remain here in the damp. She must get up, go back to Barri's. Hasn't she had enough?

She is crying deeply, violently. If she continues to the hills she will — what? Useless. Useless. Now she mutters uncontrollably, repeating that the drinking must end. How can she — and here her name, her personality, her attributes, go waving by — a woman once successful, now flayed in defeat, alone at the side of a country road as night descends around her, soaked to the bone, shivering, straining dangerously: is she the woman who once was a child bargaining with giants who strode like oriental suns, binding her to their beauty? Beyond her a tiny portal, a sliver of light, opens on a rise in the landscape. It beckons to her from a hill she must climb.

Are you alone yet? an ancient voice asks.

THREE || ASHRAM

O N E

YDESSA IS ROLLING out packing tape to close a box. The dispenser wheel screeches. Wilson sits on the table, blinking. His tail slides bits of paper, bills, and cheques back and forth. On the side of the box with a black marker she writes ROGER. She places the box on top of the others stacked in the corner of the kitchen, each bearing Roger's name in her neat hand.

Possessions are illusions, so Teresa had said. Roger may not be his old sweaters, but from the stack of them she can hear him mutter, Slow down.

She thinks of the previous summer, those morning boat trips on Baptiste Lake, how on occasion her mind would quiet, ripple, at peace, as the waves rolled serenely beneath the boat — an elegant sound slapping beneath her feet as she held the gunwales. It is blue on the lake, as her living mind is, momentarily, blue.

And what of the clinging that disrupts such peace, what of the sorrow? Who will she be without these sweaters, this condominium, the gorgeous Wilson? She has sold the condo, is putting her things in storage, has given up the real estate. She is trading the golden girl for no one. Ydessa Bloom: no one.

Everything has drained out of an existence she now repudiates. Reckless homelessness is assured. Her mind is running like an over-heated machine.

The blue sky clouding over, her bittersweet mood is gone. Nine o'clock. She's been up for hours packing things to give to Rose. Rose will decide what can go to the Hadassah. In the pre-dawn there was a vital peace that now dissolves and seeps out into the traffic that has become an irritating noise below. Behind the peace, an image of Roger had appeared. Is he still here? *Had* he been here while she packed? He had not. No, he was not here. She reaches, the spirit world does not reach back. She calls out, the spirit world does not reply. Someone she once was is elsewhere, perhaps even dead. Today there is nothing to reach for and nowhere to seek. Back when she was kick-starting each day with booze, she had chosen, if choice it had been, the questionable but lovely sensation of a mind released and floating. Hadn't the booze been a weight to hold her feet to the ground, dragging heavily, while her mind became weightless, free to drift? And now for weeks she has been refusing drink.

She thinks of all the directions into which she might go. Go in prayer and in praise, Teresa had said.

Praise what? Ydessa asked.

Start with your mother, Teresa replied.

Somewhere twenty men die of AIDS, bloodless and wasted. She thinks of this, she laments. Somewhere a poor mother sinks down, furious, defeated, on a threadbare couch, holding an unjustified bill that can't be paid. Somewhere all that sings leaps up in exaltation, but O the misery, that the singing might fall on deaf ears.

Somewhere a plane falls out of the sky.

All the effort in the human world, all the failure, it all begins to sound a clearer note. She strains to hear it. Somewhere all the misery of the world, ineluctable, a great inflammation of nerves and moving atoms, makes her go limp. Her entire body surges toward a shape curved like a rolling ball that can't be grasped, can't be gained. She falls to her knees.

Praise what?

A great grief splits her mind that seeks to shift it behind her, get everything that ails her *behind*. Who splits grief into success and failure? Who observes how the ball rolls further away, out of reach? Move beyond it. *Get over it*. Her knees ache, she has to change position.

Stacked, one box atop another, the solid word ROGER repeats in the corner of the room. What is it, pounding against her solid wall, trying to force open a window? She knows only this: she who left here last June is leaving still. Who can say she hasn't always been leaving? She grips the hardwood, exhausted.

Her body is an egg, cracking. Her tears are pooling on the floor.

Ydessa!

Rose. She drops to her knees beside her daughter.

Ydessala! Honey! The grip!

To join the tears at the back of her throat comes a cough, then a choking laugh. She sits back on her heels. Her mother's eyes are milky blue.

I have the Kleenex, Rose says, reaching for her purse.

Her mother rises, wipes dust from the knees of her slacks. She pulls a Kleenex from its pack. She surveys the table where Wilson is crouching, his tail twitching, the envelopes sliding around. Lowball and martini glasses are stacked next to a pile of old newspapers, an empty cardboard box, a Sharpie. The tower of boxes in the corner shouts ROGER.

I let myself in. Your father's checking the engine. He's telling me he's hearing things. He'll carry out your boxes, he can help in a minute. You relax. Just relax.

Ydessa blows her nose. Rose goes into the hall.

After the parents are gone, she fetches her jacket and leaves the condo, locking the door with its Judas hole, the small eye that distorts what it reveals. The glassy towers on King Street sparkle in autumn sun. A flare in her dark glasses — she looks up at the towers hot with reflected sunlight. She walks with hands in her pockets, head down, flash then down. At Bathurst she turns north, walking quickly, kicking the occasional pebble.

A streetcar rumbles past. A woman walking a small dog seems almost to say hello as she passes, but at the last second changes her mind. Two ragged men are drinking side by side in a bus shelter, passing a bottle between them. A stray dog crouches then bolts, a thin yellow line of piss drains away from her.

At Dundas she heads east, winding through the streets behind Western Hospital into Kensington Market. In a small park two Dobermans loose and on the run leap over beds of golden asters. Their owner sits reading in full sunshine on a park bench, absorbed and oblivious. The market is already busy, though it's only ten o'clock. Sun worshippers occupy the stools of a small coffee kiosk, their bodies angled each to each, heliotropic. Rays of morning sun, a chorus line of dazzle spots, are reflected in dark glasses. The proprietor of a fruit and nut stand calls out to her. Ydessala, I have those figs you like! She keeps on walking. In this way she sees how she can go forward to the ashram and leave behind what once had called to her.

James Burns is a man in his early fifties, balding, ashamed of his bald spot so he touches his head often, compulsively. In his large office a swivel chair and desk dominate the room. He levels quick questions at Ydessa, entering her answers into his computer. Worries his skull, wants only Yes, No.

You'll be all right, he says finally, all right for years. You'll see new flow with adjustments to your mixed investments. Your own spending is to be limited, you say?

He swivels, clasping his hands lightly behind his head.

No more Armani. You'll have to wear Calvin Klein.

Laughing, his small mouth full of perfect teeth.

As she walks south on Spadina past butchered carcasses of chicken and pig hanging upside down in the windows of China-town, an old woman mending a net catches her eye. Hello, old woman, she says. To give up the condo had been difficult. To leave Wilson with a friend of her parents an agony. The paradox of letting go while maintaining a tight grip.

Armani. Idiot.

She would like to collapse this world of money and glass towers and idiotic accountants and lawyers into something resembling Barri's life. A more serene life, less jarring, less troubled by empty preoccupations. The furious activity that has dominated her life has come to seem so unimportant. She can't pretend to be an old fishmonger, but neither can she be a millionaire.

She will head to the ashram in Vermont, hoping to put an end to this disquiet.

If you feel the pull to follow a dead thing and if your bones are not too weak to resist, you must resist. From this instruction, have faith softly follows. Have faith, we say, we who do not know what it is to lose a self. Put your worldly possessions in storage, ask a stranger to mind your cat, retreat for a year to an unfamiliar universe, in order, this time, to truly learn what Teresa had urged, how to breathe across thresholds.

T W O

BISEXUAL: FOR THREE years the word whirled below her polished surface. When Roger was away she would pick the word up secretively and examine it. Why marry a man who shows such impartiality? She had asked herself that, feeling in some danger of lunacy. A husband capable of loving a man and a woman, equally.

The wedding was to be the event that put questions to rest, Ydessa in her mid-length evening dress of iridescent green-gold, Roger in his silver suit. Marry. Live together. Sleep and wake together. Why would a gay husband be any sort of deprivation?

She was so unprepared for the unexpected.

His beauty was his carapace, both problem and solution. The decision to marry him was hard, yes, but was arrived at from the trust that he would never withhold anything from her. Marriage after he willingly exposed his tender underside. His vulnerability excited them. Hers she successfully kept to herself.

But what is one failure in a lifetime of failures? She turns in her bed, restless, rolling, damp, desiring home while home flaunts its Sold sign. The night will assume its own direction and find its dreams as it goes, dreams now bitter, now sweet.

———

What of three thousand and one nights? Rolling, rolling inex-pressibly, stars in a library of stars, misery come laughing at her, straining, three thousand and one nights, sleep hovering on a brink in which owls plummet in stealth, in silence, to pluck from night grass a snake sliding unawares.

At the ashram, it seems at first as if nothing is happening, as if the nights are filling with impasse and restriction only, that the nothing which comes and goes, which airs out her waiting, shows patience to be nothing but a curse, a guru's taunt, a restrictive, broken impossibility of space, which will not contain her obstacles, which leaks and drains her of blossoming thirsts and hungers. The nothing which comes and goes at first seems all.

To drink something, please.

To eat something, I beg of you.

Fill her nothing nights with a nourishment not of her own yearning.

At first her belly rejects the new food. A new life begins, but not in delight. Where is the reason? Who decided it was here she was travelling to?

Are my symptoms perhaps the symptoms of underlying disease?

The teacher laughs when she asks. No, no.

Her hands and her guts fill then empty, emptying of weight, filling with heat, with urge. I want and I want. Is this normal, this perverse sensuality? Every evening, she inclines her being to the urges of desire, a desire she is instructed to sit in, to observe. To show forbearance. She obsesses about the ice cream parlour in town. She learns that Scotch is just another kind of sugar, a glass of its honey just a picture that, once apparent in her mind, will stir the blood to a furious craving, which will always fail her — Always? Yes, *always* — again and again, fail her as surely as any ice cream.

She doesn't go to town.

Whatever you are feeling at any given moment, the guru says, whatever feelings you have at any given moment, that is what is present. And you must know that what is present here and now is you. When your intellect is sharp enough to catch what I am saying, you'll be able to do the practice, which is to be fully awake to what is.

Keep externals very simple and plain, he says. This allows the responses of your heart and mind to show up in greater detail, with more energy. You think you are here to learn how to accept the fact of life's sorrows, and maybe you are. But periods of sorrow and fear will come repeatedly. These will still be yours, and when these periods arrive you will feel isolated and lonely, possibly even betrayed. Yoga and meditation will ask you to surrender repeatedly, to persevere through every kind of restlessness you can imagine. Resistance may continue off the mat. At these times it will be important for you to seek out someone who, in your mind, is an example of wise expression, a person who speaks with grace and is not afraid to say he does not know.

Merlyn. Henry.

Ydessa asks, Are you this person?

He answers: By your blood and its circulating rhythms you will know whom it is you must seek.

But that seems already a rhythm of imitation.

Be fully here, *right now*. Be in the body. Be in the breath. Be in this moment exactly as it is and not as you would like it to be.
Breathe.
Relax.
Feel.
Watch.
Allow.

Scan the body looking for sensation: Do your muscles feel tight, are there aches or pains in the joints? Are you afraid? Is your stomach clenched? Encourage these areas to soften, to let go.
Relax, toes.
Relax, arches.
Relax, heels.
Relax, ankles.
Scan your body, from the tips of your toes to the top of your head, observing sensation, both gross and subtle. Be in the breath.

———

All goes onward and outward, nothing collapses,
And to die is different from what anyone supposed, and luckier.
After Teresa's death, you consider luck. Luck, the sheer immensity of the idea — your thinking bogs down many times. You whose life is unstructured make new efforts to give it structure. You close Teresa's house, pack up her yoga studio, drive around the county to distribute things of Teresa's that might be useful to others. You can think of nowhere to donate the prayer bells until one day a shy student phones to ask if she might have some keepsake of Teresa's. She accepts the tingsha with deep gratitude, saying, This is an instrument that tunes us.

You walk around to the far side of Baptiste, past the boys' camp to a fishing lodge set back among tall pines. The grasses are alive with Indian paintbrush, their vibrant orange blossoms flicker in strong wind and sun. At the lodge, you take the path to the shore, finding there a rowboat tied by a brass ring to a small dock. You pull the rope knot free and step into the boat. A blue jay screeches.

Rough on the lake.

You peer ahead through mounting waves, squinting in the bright light, as the boat is tossed across ridges of water. What is that ahead? Yes, yes, not a dark swell but a black horse, rising out of the churning waters, voluptuous, overwhelming. Its spray is wide, golden, dazzling, awash in monstrous light.

The horse is rearing in crescendos of liquid light. The lake is crack-ling. It teems with washed bone, a thousand bleached skulls and hooves bashing together, clattering and seething in water that floods with sorrow, bones forced through porous shell, through claw and clay, like blood gone hard white. A crackling line like a bright stairway appears, a flare, a golden line. Rider and horse break out of the welter as one. You struggle to hold your thighs and legs tight to those powerful flanks, gripping the mane, climbing, ascending the golden line that is carrying you out of the chatter, the pandemonium, into now frigid air. Winter, which flies into spring, lake ice breaking up, wind lifting.

Ice goes out in an instant and behind it crocuses instantly bloom. Skull and bone is now gull and loon on and above the shining waters. You are thrown violently through the air, falling, falling, then sliding on your knees across wet grass till you fetch up at the foot of a massive tree. Where is the hand that held tightly the luxurious mane, the pounding heart, and the strangled voice in the mind calling Help?

Jewels radiate from the spreading branches like light through stained glass. Beyond the sparkling tree is a passageway.

Your voice.

You lift from your knees to a lustrous, jewelled landscape.

In thin morning light you wake, exhaling in small bubbles. *Put, put.* Even recovering from a series of late nights, you rarely sleep in past five o'clock. 6:03 a.m. You will make a fire. You shake off phantom energy, brief tremors, a dream. You move in the dim light without hesitation, you know your rooms, having walked alone in and out of them for so many years in the house your father built. A shadow is clinging. You shake it off.

You restack three logs that have tumbled, carry kindling to the stove, flip up the latch, crouch in front of the open box, crumple sheets of newspaper, add kindling. You strike a match on the stone floor, flame flares up. Moonlight shines clear on the lake. The fog has cleared.

Fire takes hold, the flames eat smoke, you attend the swift heat. The rolling world takes with it every person you have ever loved. You bend to observe the fire through the glass, beautiful and exact, all tenderness. You welcome the heat. You close the stove door, stand, and stretch your arms above your head as Teresa taught you to do, waking the body in careful accretions, reaching first your right arm and then your left into the space above your head, feeling the stretch along your ribs. With both arms still raised you join your palms, exhale, then bend your knees, and hold the pose — *Utkatasana* — for one minute. Fierce pose. You lower your arms. The action tells you how you can go.

In the kitchen, on the counter, is the ashtray Teresa always used.

Observe the breath as it enters at the base of the nostrils.

How is it?

Breathe.

Relax.

Feel.

Observe.

Allow.

Where in your body are you keeping tight hold on life? Can you let go a little? The moment you realize that your mind has wandered is the moment when you are most conscious, that is the moment to bring your attention back to the breath. Observe the breath as it enters the body, observe the breath as it exits the body, pay attention to the sensations at the base of the nostrils, even as wind bangs the shutter and shadows draw out across the floor.

Self-observation without judgement will be practiced on and off the mat. Asking yourselves why you came here, why you are here, questioning yourself: this will happen. Did you come here of your own free will, or did someone send you? Yoga is not a substitute for knowledge, not an alternative to asking hard questions about life's meaning and direction and the goals of your existence. You must work through your suffering. Yes, the first step truly is to awaken out of long years of sleep, but that is only the beginning. Look, I'm telling you, some huge, some giant force is going to try to eat you, and not only once but many times, millions of times. You are going to be asked to stay present while dangling in the jaws of that giant force, in the dead of night, alone and without aid. You will be asked to be fully aware of your self *without judgement* in that most threatening moment when to be fully here, in the moment *as it is*, will feel like death. You think you're up to it. But why would you even want to be?

THREE

DEAR BARRI,

How can a woman reach her thirties without noticing how in childhood we are each given a code, a code unwittingly absorbed by mimicking parents, whose own codes were uncritically absorbed by watching their parents? After weeks of practice here at the ashram I have begun to understand that my movements and habits of mind and body express a persistent effort to alleviate instantly any and all misgivings: in short, to flee. To hide. Or, if I can't do either, to resist. To denounce. My teacher has likened this noisy effort to the gossip mill. Pay no attention! He likens fear to a creature whose tools are these: it talks fast and gets in our face. Listen, he says, but try not to follow it, certainly do not believe it. Nothing is what it seems. And there are ways each of us has of refusing to comprehend this nothing.

To be resident here requires that I make a vow of celibacy, obedience, and simplicity. The code is made explicit. Here, this code, these vows, are not difficult. The hardest thing will be to keep up my practices on my return to Toronto. I'm thinking of returning next fall, but this could change. Whenever I do return, the peaceful qualities of my life here, its surprising serenity, will,

I expect, vanish like a dream. Everyone who enters the departure lounge, as it is called here, seems to start again to complicate their lives unnecessarily.

Me? Will I take up complaining? Whenever I think of complainers I think of Rose. These thoughts unfold in the theatre of my mind. My parents are not to blame for the wreck I have made of things. I remember this, then I forget.

It has been a strangely private time, surrounded by one hundred other practitioners, a time during which I catch myself trying *not* to remember you or Baptiste. We rise every morning at four, wash and dress while the sky is still dark, and move in silence to the sanctuary as the gong rings, to take our places there, to wait for our guru, who leads us in morning meditation. The thoughts that come after months of effort have not much to do with Roger or Teresa or you or Henry. The white robes we wear, the cult-like atmosphere, the silence expected of us, the extreme rules of behaviour, the pain roiling in my hips as I sit in the lotus position: these are the thoughts that come. I'm asked to talk difficulties over with my teacher, to disallow negativity and cynicism to develop. I notice small movements, small sounds and smells, but these don't occupy me very much, nor cause me to wonder about them.

Perhaps everything that has happened has forever altered my capacity for wonder. Or maybe only few of us are as highly sensitive as Henry. I notice things in the corners of my eyes, but I keep my gaze forward or down, just as we are instructed to do. I watch my mind as it empties and fills, empties and fills. It's a river that throws itself over an escarpment, endlessly cascading, nothing more.

Once a week we are asked to thoroughly clean our small rooms then move on to the halls and meeting areas with our buckets of hot water, our brushes and cloths. Talk is permitted during the performance of these weekly chores. Talk, or song. Otherwise we conduct our days in what is called noble silence. Times to meet individually with the guru have been offered. These are not obligatory. Mostly I stay on my own: this will likely come as no surprise to you.

The hours of silence as Henry worked on his elaborate drawings — maybe I should have studied him more closely, invited him in more often, no matter what the consequences might have been.

Through the open windows of the sanctuary comes the sound of two gardeners raking leaves on the lawn, the scrape of metal teeth across hard earth, rhythmic and welcome. Most of the songbirds have gone now, and Ydessa, as she lies in Savasana, is aware of how she misses them, how she is counting the days until their return next spring. Her hips ache. She wonders if she has sustained an injury and whether or not she should be pulling back from even the simplest poses, like *Padahastasana*. The man on the mat next to hers is fussing with a blanket he has gracelessly unfolded, groaning slightly as he shakes it out over his now-supine body. A woman on the mat next to him is singing quietly under her breath. These irritations swirl amid the quiet morning while the sun pours through the windows and the gardeners continue to pull their rakes across the earth, the guru sensing everything in his lotus position, a mountain of presence on a raised throne at the front of the hall, his face serene, his eyes closed.

Wherever would she find the answer to the question, did you come here of your own volition or did compulsion send you here? A year has come and gone, yet still she asks herself why she is here. Why did she take off at a run, first to Baptiste in the moment she first learned of Roger's death, then to New York, then Baptiste again? Is she really looking for something at the retreat, or does she flee?

How shapely the days had once been, days when she climbed out of bed while Roger was still stirring, to make coffee in the kitchen, wash and dress, then drive to the office, where she handled multiple requests to meet, show, sell, advocate, strategize, to lie (yes), to adorn, and (yes, yes) make nice. There was a hurry to those days that she thought quite wonderful. Here the call is to slow, stop, still, to quiet: to refrain from reaching, from grasping.

These library shelves with their books on ashram lineage, Ayurvedic yoga, dharmic practice, meditation, mindfulness, and self-improvement, she scans them for some story that might hold her attention effortlessly. Grief still threatens to swamp her. The freedom that had been hers, to choose her day, her hour, her own reading — Chekhov, Virginia Woolf — is now refused. Who is to blame for this loss? When her teacher said that a giant would show up to eat her, she had not imagined a beast who might take the shape of a closed book, reading denied, choice of what to read, artists and their words refused. She had not imagined a beast come to tear from her the pleasure of immersion in old stories. These new stories ask only one question, or so it seems to her: what is time?

On his twelfth birthday, his father gives over to him the job of inspecting the bee colony. Do this every two weeks. Watch your queen, Henry. Is she laying lots of eggs? The queen can lay up to three thousand eggs a day. Check for mites or other pests. Do you remember what I told you about the Varroa mite?

In winter he likes to prepare the syrup to feed the bees. Bees don't sleep, but they stay in the hive, moving upward, eating their own stores. He likes to stand next to the winter hive, wrapped in its cover, the bees sleepless inside. The librarian at his school recommends that he read Rilke.

Your doubt may become a good quality if you train it. It must become knowing, it must become critical. Ask it, whenever it wants to spoil something for you, why something is ugly, demand proofs from it, test it, and you will find it perplexed and embarrassed perhaps, or perhaps rebellious. But don't give in, insist on arguments and act this way, watchful and consistent, every single time, and the day will arrive when from a destroyer it will become one of your best workers — perhaps the cleverest of all that are building your life.

To summon doubt this way, to call it a destroyer and then to overlay an image of worker bees on top of doubt. Clever bees, building his life.

Her room is the size of a cell — small single bed with clean starched linens, small white wooden dresser with two drawers — and yes, she minds this scaled-down living, she who brought herself here. Obviously the answer to the question is, *She* chose this. Assiduously chose it, closing down one life and taking up another.

Residents are asked to meditate on and off the mat, to walk mindfully pretty much anywhere they go, whether to the sanctuary or by the side of the lake or in the labyrinth, in the dining hall with the others, eating together in devotional silence.

Watch your breath.

Observe your feelings.

If you feel angry or restless, that is not you. You might feel like a failure. That is *not* you. What is present at any given time *is* you.

The paradox — free to leave at any time and yet trapped — often makes her chest heave with emotion. Drink? No. Not free to drink. She craves sugar. Her body longs to lie in the maw of booze, and yes, that is one way to go, but she has pledged to find another. She may be going nowhere, but she's going to arrive not drunk but sober. *Awake*, as the teachers like to say.

She is assigned a young teacher, whose name is Rass. Now I suggest you just relax, he instructs. Breathe in through your nose, breathe out through your mouth, and make your breathing go out long and steady, as if you are breathing out through a straw. Again breathe in. Breathe out. Continue that a few times.

The purpose is to relax. Breathe in through the nose, and when you breathe out make it prolonged. Allow it to feel as a kind of physical emptying, as well as emptying your mind of all expectations, so that you are really entering a state of non-doing.

You may close your eyes.

Continue to breathe.

Now bring your attention to the spot between your eyebrows and be completely at peace with who you are. Be content with what you are doing, so that your breath becomes very shallow, soft, and when you come to your third eye, the spot between your eyebrows, you will be calm and deeply relaxed.

Allow yourself to enter into a place of complete stillness.

Keep your attention on the third eye and feel the energy that has been activated by the breath.

Allow your attention to drop down into sensations that are stirred up through your breath, and do not choose For or Against.

Remain in a feeling space.

You have dropped down from thinking to feeling. Go deeper into feeling.

Feel what you are feeling rather than have any feelings about your feelings. Now that you have entered into your feeling centre, be totally present with what is as is.

Relax into it.

Let go.

Let go of all doing.

Feel that energy in your arms and throughout your whole body as a sitting energy field. Feel it in your arms, feel it in your face, feel it in your body, and know that this pulsation is in perfect rhythm with your heart.

And now that you are so deeply relaxed, now that you do not have the boundaries of your body on your mind, let your energy field merge with the cosmic energy field. Extend your awareness, embrace the whole unconditionally.

Remain with this through all that comes through the field of your awareness. Just listen to the sound of Om.

And feel it, because now you are fully present in your feeling, in your heart centre.

Om.

Om.
Om.
Now bring your awareness back to your body.
You may gradually open your eyes.

FOUR

O GRIEVOUS, NEFARIOUS, inimical world. Weep, with head hung down, weep, thoughtless and free in the starless night. Ydessa's agony goes unnoticed, her fear unremarked. She should bolt and keep on running. She will never gain the peace that comes with understanding. Peace is for others, never her.

She moves to the sanctuary, to her place on her mat, and awaits further instructions.

From Vajrasana, exhale slowly as you hinge at your hips. Bring your forehead down to touch your mat. Move your hands over your head into *Anjali Mudra*. Relax your frontal brain. We'll continue in a flow: lift up, bringing your hands up overhead, palms together, returning to Vajrasana.

We'll be in this flow for one hundred and eight rounds.

He is asked to stay back after class. His teacher wants to know if she may see his drawings. An art show is being planned.

Bring ten or so to school tomorrow.

They are only sketches.

She waits. Finally she says, Will you say more?

My mother gave me a chart of the solar system. She told me that the limits of the universe are not known.

Yes? Go on.

There may be no other place like Earth. I try to sketch its beauty.

She pushes a little more. For example?

He looks around the classroom. For example, gold shafts of sunlight. He adds, I'd like to see the Atlantic Ocean one day. I'd like to see Venice one day. But for now gold shafts will have to do. And it is impossible to draw them. The moment I try to draw anything of beauty, a breach opens up.

She is told to meet with the guru. She is allowed to say something or nothing, as she wishes. He talks. Small talk. Large talk.

When you accept what is present *at this moment*, then all that is not real automatically becomes disengaged from your attention. Whatever is superimposed over the present gets disconnected. Do you catch that? Avoiding what is will only result in restlessness, an inability to inhabit your body. Do not feign composure, as I see you so often do. Do not feign confidence. Do not make the mistake so many others have made, Ydessa. When you fall out of bliss, don't try to get back in.

———

Table.
    Bed.
    Light.
    Memory.
    Henry. Barri. Teresa.
    A disturbance in the breath.
    I am.

What keeps you going when the going gets hard? You don't have to stay here, you've plenty of money. What keeps you coming back to your mat?

Sometimes my mind settles in practice. Sometimes I am not a cauldron.

A cauldron. Say more about this, please.

Sometimes my husband comes. He sits next to me. He is quiet and respectful. My thoughts are not disturbed by his presence. I am not disturbed by thoughts about metaphysics, about the impossibility of Roger being there, sitting next to me as I move through the postures. I feel sad, certainly. Tears pour down my face. But sometimes my mind settles. Sometimes I'm peaceful.

The day has been dark — low skies, fog, and drizzle — the mood sombre among the residents. As the community gathers for its evening satsang, an unusual silence wraps the room. She notices the anxious silence then lets it go.

Someone has forgotten to bring matches. Ydessa volunteers to fetch a box from housekeeping, glad for the chance to escape the company's grey atmosphere. As she moves down the cold halls, drawing her fingertips along its surfaces, heading for the stairwell, she notices again a tinnitus that has been playing loud in her ears, and beneath that buzz familiar haunting chords from the sound-track of *Apocalypse Now*. Beautiful friend.

She knows these halls well, keeps her eyes closed for the game of it.

Breathe.

Relax.

Feel.

Watch.

Allow.

All day she has been given to a strange fear accompanied by the sad and spectral music of Jim Morrison and The Doors. She makes an effort to allow the aural hallucination, tries neither to egg it on nor savage it. Her fingers are reading the walls, feet stepping adroitly, if blindly. She does not turn on the lights.

Boxes of matches wrapped in cellophane are kept in a cup-board above a small sink. She stops to wash her hands, remembering Rose, how during childhood she told Ydessa, Soap up for as long as it takes to say one verse of any Sinatra song. She soaps her hands as helicopters land in the killing fields of Cambodia. *This is the end, beautiful friend, the end.* The tinnitus is droning, hot.

She is moving in the unlit hallway when she hears voices. The sounds do not register at first, having been playing alone in the dark a gambit of perilous threat over an abyss. She stops, opens her eyes. It is the guru, laughing with the woman they call Ambica. Their voices are strange in the grim evening, sensuous and bright, warm as the sun. Intimate. Or is it conspiratorial?

Just looking for the light, she says awkwardly as they pass.

She has resumed her place on her mat. The guru is back on his platform, asking participants to meditate on the deepest aspect of themselves. They chant together. You are sky. You are that which moves through changeless sky. You are wind and weather, sun, moon. You are day and cloud, night and star.

Like every participant at the ashram, she is reminded that to converse with others about the guru's habits and movements is not allowed. In light of what she has just seen and heard, she recalls the pledge. He sits on his throne before the assembled.

People tend to think that yoga and asana are one and the same. No. What are you doing on your mat? Have you asked yourself this question? Some of you have been here for months, some of you for years. Have you asked yourself this question?

He is spoiling for argument, wants to bring fire into the hall.

Who can tell me what is the purpose of moving through the poses? Some people think asana is an end in itself. No. Asana frees the energy in the body from ego mind that tries to contain it, so that you can awaken. To practice poses without consciousness is to refuse the tool of prana. Isn't that so? He surveys his audience. Ydessa, what do you say?

She does not answer, so he repeats, louder this time.

Is what I say true, Ydessa?

She wants to stand, to be visible to him at least. To be fifteen rows back, unseen, understood to be in her place, a place assigned, drawn on a sanctuary map given to her on arrival, her acquiescence to that small place assured, to be that far back is horrible.

I do not hear your answer, he shouts.

She rises.

Yes, I believe you once said that to practice poses without consciousness is like owning a hammer but not using it to build a house.

Good. Does everyone else catch that? Now sit down, Ydessa, and try to be less creative about the ways you seek to gain attention. If you stand up again so that you stand out, you go back to zero. To show off is ego mind.

After midnight. She has not slept, though she has been in her room since nine. Lying there, her breathing an exercise she has kept up for over three hours, counting each inhalation, each exhalation, noting the colour of each, the texture, the depth — staying her course. She will not become agitated, because that is the work, isn't it? To stay one's ground, to keep one's equanimity, the mind filling up with thoughts and words that pass away, the ten thousand things of this present moment rolling in concealed anguish, cascading in denied fury, her sky, star, and centre, humiliated, and her Self, that which *is*. How dare he. She could smash him.

In the morning her sheets are soaked with sweat.

To make renewed effort will not be easy. She is not on familiar terms with the kind of flexibility renewed effort requires, but her teacher has said you cannot split god. He is in the dung heap as surely as in the palace.

Okay, get up, god.

She sighs.

You and I, your palace and my dung heap, are going for a walk in the labyrinth, not to morning practice. Earth time, god. Body time. Let's get a little control over our breath. Let's get back to the practice while we check out the garden.

At the gate she sees how the rising sun strikes shadow across the radiant valley. Hoping to catch something of it, letting dung or palace choose, she relaxes her hold on her thoughts.

Let's go in. We've always got time for a pranayama walk, right? Mindful walk. Ebb and flow. Systole and diastole. In sun-bright quickened breath, shuddering. Shouldn't seeing be reacting by now? She regards her thoughts. No more wow.

The path twists.

Can more breath — in the spot at the back of the head?

She sends breath from her rib cage to her skull.

More yellow goat's beard, gaywings, small wildflowers. She is naming flowers. She observes her knowledge of names. Showoff, no more wow. A volt shoots up her spine. Muscles to slacken.

Can burn the paper proclaim yourself slack like an unbroken pouring of oil. *Dirgha*.

You clavicle rib belly.

You no thing.

Here comes Tiger safe.

Sam and Rose visit the ashram. It is spring, and the foliage on the hills is celery green.

You look so well, Poppa.

Seventy. Someone said seventy's the new fifty. This means

what, Ydessala? That I'm ready now for the new mid-life crisis? For the inner revolution? For a zonk I am most days ready: a zonk. Anytime, a zonk.

Poppa.

How she liked long ago to correct his English, his malapropisms, taking perverse pleasure in her instruction. How he had embarrassed her, made her feel too exposed. She retaliated, made a proud career out of scorn, expressing what was weak or weakening in both of them. She was quick to notice failure, quick to notice flaws, quick to cast shadows. Once, sitting poolside in the company of an old family friend, she donned a pair of her mother's pink mules and wiggled her toes, unexpectedly, sarcastically, in the hot afternoon sun, watching the feathers lift and sigh. The old friend observed her.

Looks like you want a kind of Father-Knows-Best. You want a Donna Reed. They are survivors, Ydessa. They still fear they might lose everything. They're doing their level best. It's quite wrong of you to insist on these hurtful experiments. Try to be less preoccupied with trivialities.

At sixteen, in the year of deepest shame — pink downy feathers adrift across the too-green lawn, Sinatra records playing, a small repertoire of bad jokes badly told — she learned for the first time of her father's incarceration at Dachau, learned from this old trusted friend that her father had turned sixteen while confined there. She had done the math too late.

It is said, Rass tells her, that there's no value in digging shallow wells in a hundred places. Decide one place and dig deep. Even if you encounter a rock, use dynamite and keep going down. If you leave that well to dig another, all the first effort is wasted, and there is no proof you won't hit rock again.

Tell that to the man on Baptiste Lake who spent a fortune digging without ever hitting water.

What I am saying is, it is within your good nature, if you persist, that you will find water.

THE HOUSE THEY stumble on in their short stroll away from the ashram is well hidden at the end of a muddy driveway. On its collapsed porch a disintegrating brown couch is sinking into the concrete. Most of the ceiling tiles have fallen, the roof has rotted out. An early pantry addition has collapsed and blocks the back door. Plants are growing in muddy bedrooms. Strips of Green Lantern wallpaper droop above ardent life rising out of the soil on what was once a child's bedroom floor.

This abandoned life outside the borders of the ashram.

Rose asks questions about the area. Ydessa cannot answer. She has never gone beyond the gates. How do you know so little about this place, Rose asks, you with your thirsty mind? You always want to know it all. You have stayed in this prison all these years even though you are no prisoner? Even though you are free to leave anytime? Sam, tell her something smart.

But it's enough to sit by the lake or walk the labyrinth, Momma. Much more than enough. Just to watch the changes that every day brings is enough.

Pish.

They are teaching me to get out of myself. You can understand this?

To go where, exactly, if you go nowhere?

The teachers say, You are not your feelings in any present moment. You are what you observe in any present moment.

So you are persuaded to be a lake? Here we are a decrepit house?

Ha. Sam laughs. Good one, Rose. Ydessa's teachers got you there. He turns to his daughter. Turns out we *are* a decrepit house. The stairs are too hard for your mother, and I can't find the enthusiasm the pool requires. Our neighbours are strangers with young children. It's time. We've sold the house, Ydessala, to a young couple. Nice people. We are moving to a residence on Bathurst.

A residence.

Yes. Where your mother won't have to cook.

What's it like?

Expensive.

Oh. Do you need money, Poppa? I can give —

Hush. No. We do not need your money.

Rose shouts, Roger's money! A whore's money!

Stop it, Rosie. No. It's not Roger's money. It's Ydessala's money.

Three years only she knew him and his money. Now it's hers?

It was what Roger wanted, Rosie. His will said so, not only the law.

Her mother turns to Ydessa. Your teachers are right. You looked at Roger and now you are his money.

Her parents gone, she is in a meeting with Rass. What I'm talking about is devotion. The tools we take into devotion on the mat are postures, their flow and prana. The tools we use off the mat are nonviolence, truth, non-thieving, non-covetousness, and, for single people like yourself, celibacy.

I haven't wanted sex in almost four years.

And yet your period of restraint could suddenly end.

This seems unlikely. Her ashram bed is a winter lake with prism sails.

Your mother is very important to you. You needed more warmth and support from your parents than you received, and you often felt you were not getting enough. That feeling continues, yes?

My father wants me to accept some things from their house. I don't want anything. When Sam begins to itemize the so-called alluring things I must surely want, my mother interrupts him to say, I spend a life getting these nice things, so Ydessa gets them overnight? But to say No is to insult her, to show again how little I love what she has struggled to give me.

For weeks now Rass had been asking questions about the months following Roger's death. Were you unable to part with many of your possessions before coming here? he asks. You sold your condo, yes, and you let go of your dear pet. But many things you stored somewhere, is that correct?

My parents disturb me, that is certain, and possessions can disturb me, yes. True. But my possessions are not parent substitutes.

You are sure about this? Sometimes in life we are consumed with a sharp foreboding. Sometimes before or after a great loss we acquire or dispose of things recklessly. We think that possessions will soften life, make life easier. Or we think being free of possessions will soften us. What softness did you think millions of dollars would give you? Or do you imagine giving your money away? Money has betrayed you, you think, just like Rose and

Sam. But having or not having is not the problem. Making room for what *is* is what has to be.

At Baptiste Lake an owl leaves its roost, plummets, eyelids shuttering, closing in on its prey. A yellow finch cries. You sit by the window, listening for something as the hour goes by. Then you pick up your brush and utter a line of violet paint on the paper balanced on your lap. You close your eyes. The sounds of the lake open steadily. You open your eyes. Now a line of pink on the lower half of the paper.

You think of the owl. In pellets you found beneath the roosting boughs, tiny spaces and grooves were jammed with feathers and bones, hair wound tight into cavities of tiny bird skulls.

A wash of white, a grey materializes.

The lake, which is a mirror, Anchorwoman, who is ornate, the neurological functions in their accretions, the busted *samskaras*, and those yet to bust.

Palest blue. Pale salmon. More violet. Pewter.

Challenge, return, intellectualization, want, innovation.

Fear.

Flush the resistance with cold water.

S I X

YES, THAT WAS the kind of car she drove, Henry thinks, standing over a Corvette parked outside the old theatre in Picton. A red Corvette convertible. He can remember Ydessa at the wheel, driving fast, can see the figure of himself as a child, walking in a daydream haze by the side of the road. The figures come easily to him. Twelve years have passed since that astonishing summer, when, for a time, he felt his mother had beheld him whenever he was in Ydessa's company.

He looks at the passenger seat as meaning shifts, strong emotion winding back through time to that summer when he was nine. He can see Ydessa, how stern she looks. He must have seen her like that, looking away from him toward the shoreline, yes, in Barri's beautiful mahogany boat, the motor softly humming as he took up his pen and held it horizontal, as Barri — or someone else? who? — had instructed him to do, measuring the width of Ydessa's cheeks, her cheekbones and ears, her face, and below the bones the nostrils and lips. Start by finding the shape of the face then begin in the middle, placing the eyes — who had shown him how? He had turned his pen aright, bent over his paper and watched as the portrait came alive beneath his hand, not as beautiful as Ydessa, but beautiful, young, and torn.

Torn?

Yes.

Where are these drawings now? What has he done with them? He has not picked up a pen in years.

Those sketches, his little analyses of rhythm in a verdant season, patterns of insect and cloud on windless days. Baptiste Lake. He had made an effort not to think of those days. He had stopped his hand from making the effort to put down on paper the ceaseless, restless movements of the earth, the dance that was sunlight moving on a woman's face, altering its planes and angles, sunlight that widened or narrowed cheekbones above a mouth that frowned, was held tightly.

Fecund summer.

Inevitable chaos.

He turns away from the Corvette, and those memories.

Where is Ydessa Bloom?

Her figure moves before his eyes. He would like to see her, to see how she has aged. If they were to meet, he would want each to accord the other the same old measure of respect and curiosity. He recalls the shape of her with such pointed desire, such infinite loneliness. His failure to remember a figure he now sees in front of him plain as day deprives him of surety. He does not know her face, a mask of shadow and light.

From disturbance to disturbance his mind flits. The future is a threat. He shrinks from it.

He has his degree now. School is officially over. What next? He doesn't know.

He opens his eyes to the lovely figure of a woman who meant — he can't find the words. He can't begin to think of her. Events kept so far in his background that there can be no story, no memory.

Where is Ydessa now?

He knew of Teresa's cancer. He'd gone to the wall, he'd held his tongue. In fields the colour of corn and alfalfa he laid down to sleep for four thousand nights.

Whatever.

Why did Ydessa arrive at Baptiste, steal his young imagination, receive then lose his mother's ring, and leave? A total fucking travesty. What was it they had been to each other, there at that other end of his existence? Had no promises been made, to keep in touch, to call, to write? Well, what's a promise worth?

Do not deceive yourself. He knew to say this to himself. In the intervening years, except for Barri, who had come looking for him, had invited him to re-enter her life — total fucking shutout.

Dear Barri,

It's been a long while. I've had some trouble. I'm having a hard time shaking the feeling that I'm the wrong sort of human. I know that sounds melodramatic, and I know I'm basically fine, but sometimes it seems like I must be wrong. It's very inhibiting. But also I'm too stubborn to try to be any other sort of human, which is maybe a good thing.

I'm reading a book about a boy who meets a travelling theatre company. Everything I like — except the earth and sky and certain people — feels like it's from another time.

Alas for a sad little note.

Henry

FOUR || 2003

ONE

IN THE DREAM that repeats, his mother stands behind his father, who gathers and cups to his open, unprotected hands a small mudra of bees and winds them into a comb, one hand wrapping strands of honey around their bodies, startlingly yellow, bright, and buzzing, the sound enormous — she smiles at him, briefly, urging him to accept what he might not understand.

He is standing on a wooden chair with his hands in the air, drawing the release, tracing sensation in intricate detail, the perfect geometry of a father.

When Henry was five he said to his mother, I didn't know the world was real. I thought it was a giant's dream.

Did you, baby? Well, how do you know it isn't?

I can't find the staircase.

What staircase?

The one leading to his house.

His mother put her hand on his head.

Did you look in the back of the closet?

Which closet?

How do I know? All of them. I mean, maybe don't give up yet. You're only five years old.

Time is running out, was what he had said.

The world is immense, multiple, complex, sparkling, and shifting. Barrels of fossil fuel are burning, tons of carbon dioxide curling down through air, being absorbed into the atmosphere. Every day brings with it some newly extinct or threatened or endangered species, every day a pain in his chest becomes more pronounced on account of all he is forever saying goodbye to, infinitely becoming, infinitely passing away. What good was a small fountain pen against this rush of matter, against frequency and velocity, against such colossal force and dissipation?

She found the space for the Toronto studio almost immediately, but the owner, when he heard her plans, was reluctant to sell to her. This is a neighbourhood of honest working people, he said. The notion that yoga was a frivolous, bourgeois activity, a luxury, began to creep into that conversation.

When she was a child, adept at concealment from Rose most particularly, accused of cheerlessness, she sought private places where she could be alone, play quietly, read books. Inevitably Sam came looking for her, interrupting her solitude. Sensual things, their insistency breaking silence — they can't be the measure of the world. Neither can the world be measured by words. The world is not made of the din of language. So many things one feels cannot be put into words, yet the force of the wish to is enormous. The world is a giant telling, and the price it exacts for pretending otherwise is very high.

In 1999, during the time when reality TV aired a series called *The Real World*, she opened her studio. Practicing and teaching in a small, two-storey building whose windows faced west, in an area of Toronto known for absent landlords, low rents, defiance of building codes, and, most slyly, artists and their counterculture, she discovered something new about Savasana, corpse pose, the final resting pose of every yoga practice. As corporate buyers rushed to build on old corners of the city, as neighbourhood guerrilla artists articulated the city's failings, she yoked her daily breath to something almost dead within her, straining to be revived.

Yoga was by then a way of life. Buried deep in her focus on breath and in her reach for understanding of the ancient mysteries, source of modern-day yoga, she felt the obduracy of old attachments give way. Where memory could not go, into ancient crevices, things of long ago broke free. In the tender hold of a new city, awash in a great loosening, she entered revivifying waters: mid-life.

She is seated in Paschimottanasana, the forward bend, breathing deeply, directing her breath into a stitch of pain in her lower back, observing the subtle clench there, observing the muscle, its inability to relax, observing slight, slow sensation while breathing deeply, her forehead resting lightly against her shins, her blood warmed, obstacles removed or departing, and the thought comes to her: Henry. Henry Rattle. Henry.

She lets the thought go.

Briefly her heart clenches, briefly she sends her mind to her heart, and a thought comes again: his mother's ring. Henry, the boy, and she, young, Henry drawing patterns of earth and sky, of breath, pen travelling across a lake. Henry's water is blue, is green. Henry coming to see her. Henry Rattle. She lets the thought go.

As she lets the thought go, watches it depart, she lets associations come flooding in, she watches attractions come, she watches aversions come, she watches the throat's craning impulse come, lets the impulse to cry out come then go, she directs her breath to her forehead and throat, tears draw up and begin to fall, pooling and streaming in the space between her strong calves. Seated in Paschimottanasana, she observes all this, bent over in forward fold, a posture she's practiced for fifteen years. Henry is coming to see her and she will tell him that his mother's ring is never far from her thoughts, its absence is part of her, part of a haunting pattern of losses through the years. For fifteen years Henry has been her companion, Henry and the questions he used to ask. She returns to the breath, and the thoughts of Henry vanish.

The class over, the students roll up their mats. They fold their blankets, speaking uneasily to one another as they return the studio's few props to cupboards and shelves. The atmosphere is thick, a chain of linked energies pulses across the floor of the light-filled room. She watches the chain slither, snakelike and serene, seeping into the wall, wall like skin, skin like a web, energies coolly absorbed. A young woman hesitates, wishing to ask a question, unprepared to ask it and ill-prepared to receive an answer. She waits for the room to clear.

Ydessa?

Yes.

Can I talk to you?

Yes.

It's a little embarrassing.

She says nothing.

Today when we were doing *Bhastrika*, I think I had an orgasm.

You had an orgasm. Yes, that can happen.

Can it? Really?

Yes.

I was focused on my nose. My nose was like a little engine, a little animal.

The young woman looks at her, imploring. She says nothing.

It was a little embarrassing.

Was it?

I wanted it to stop.

Did you?

The young woman giggles. It was so embarrassing. Will I ever be able to do Bhastrika again? I'll always be distracted now.

Well . . .

The young woman interrupts.

I like your classes, though. I really do. I mean, thanks, Ydessa. Namaste.

———

She observes each student, each with her begging bowl. The higher values do not spring forth from obedience to a teacher like corn springing from seed in the earth. The higher values can't be taught, Rass told her. She believes she has only this quietude, this silent reception, to give.

Namaste, she says, bowing to the young woman, catching at the opening of consciousness a flash of light that is Teresa.

After ten years at the ashram, living in its concentration of mind and its cultivation of positive emotion, she wanted to return to Toronto to open a yoga studio, to teach, alone, to learn to be a good teacher within the powerful contrary demands of all that makes up one life. She believed she had developed self-restraint.

Rass had cautioned her. Monastic-minded individuals are eventually derided, certainly misapprehended, he said. Are you sure this will be the life for you?

She meditated long on the questions that arose at the ashram, still committed, disciplined, turning each question over and over. The idea of returning to Toronto was carried within her. If fear or guilt or uncertainty is to be mine, she thought, if hot emotion should enter at the base of my spine and coil there, she could, she believed, contain it.

Emotion does coil there. It dozes.

How auspicious the moment when a person who carries a burning question asks whether there might be another way to formulate the question. Do I wish to stay at the ashram for the rest of my life? Is a hermetic life the life I was given? Who benefits from my being a recluse? Between her heart of hearts and the practice and teaching of yoga lay all the world, and earth and heaven too. She came away from the ashram determined to teach, but not too much, to make offerings to eager students, but in moderation, to be available to inquiring minds, to witness as inquiring minds turned mountains upside down in order to explore the upswinging darkness. But she would not lose herself in teaching. While she admired agility and lightness in the mind and the body, at the ashram she had come to know the cost and demands of each of these, to know that lightness is a secret one must learn. She wished to remain free as the secrets continued to unfold.

She returned to Toronto four years after the ashram community had fallen apart in scandal and the guru was told to leave. She and a few others had stayed on, at first in the deepest kind of confusion. They felt that the guru had betrayed them. Those who remained made an effort to meditate, to practice honest appraisal of the heart, and to remember that disentanglements still lingered, waiting to be realized. It was an excruciating time for everyone. Everyone saw how it was that for years they had cordoned off parts of themselves that did not fit the story they wanted, parts that shamed, parts that could not be loved. Eventually some were able to open their hearts to the ways they had denied their fuller selves, and those who addressed the sensuous coiling desire that shook their bodies became more peaceful, closer to the ideal they had envisioned.

A million dollars invested, she had cried. Roger's money, given to a monster, just so I could remain in America.

Rass tried to console her. You gave that money to the ashram, not only to our guru.

But this is the argument any rationalization makes. It has to be said that Roger's money helped to further others' abuse. The sheer ignorance of it. I should have known. Deplorable.

You could not have known. On the surface of things, it looked as if our guru lived a simple life. But he was not obedient, not austere, not by a long shot.

I love to go to the market, the flimflam man had told them, boasting. I love to see all the things I can happily do without.

Whereas he had not done without — not at all — while Ydessa, in the shadows, had tried, with humour and grace, to refuse the temptations of the multifarious world.

T W O

SAM AND ROSE rise slowly from their designated table in the dining room on Bathurst Street, their moods shifting along a spectrum ranging from anger to sadness. In the elevator, and walking slowly down the hall to their three small rooms, they tell each other old jokes, though these are less entertaining than jokes once were. More tiresome. On better days they enjoy cocktails at five o'clock, but the atmosphere of defeat kept to the margins of their younger years now claims much more space, like hollows in old bones. How close each is to falling.

You think aging's easy, Ydessala. Just wait. Everything wonderful gets reduced to ice cream and naps.

Confusion lives in three small rooms. Defeat joins sorrow here, a sad harmony attends the rhythm of their days.

The ashram opened Ydessa's heart to new calculations, to measurements having to do with Rose and Sam's early adulthood, their joking voices, the bright colours of their walls, the summer pools, gin cocktails. Her mother's life, her father's life: half lives, after beginnings that had borne too much of the wrong kind of life. And this was her inheritance, this failure to learn what she understood late through the effort of meditation and yoga, this half life left to them after all the looting and thieving and humiliation that had come to a halt on VE day.

She had exchanged her parents' gin for Scotch whisky, speed for their Sinatra. She had traded in dreams, the cheerful golden girl of real estate who assured her clients that dreams come true in bigger houses. She had done these things, reached for unreliable props, laminated them. In amber liquid swirled with ice, through calculated sales pitches, bits and pieces of a stolen life. In retreat she had begun to ask after the real conditions of life, while Rass gently held her in her disintegration.

She is lighting the wicks of eight tea lights distributed every four centimetres along the mantelpiece of the former fireplace of this old tailor shop. This is her studio in Little Portugal on a street teeming with activity. If one knows where to look, and how to look, one can detect a palimpsest of the tailor's working life. *We are only lightly covered with buttoned cloth; and beneath these pavements are shells, bones, and silence.*

No student has asked about the mending that once took place in these small rooms. Tony, once the owner, opened the shop in 1950. He ran a thriving business with his young wife and two teenaged boys. But first one son and then the other moved away, moved west, following enticements. No one in the extended family showed any interest in the business. Too much work, too few rewards.

A yoga studio?

Tony knew of no Portuguese, no Italian, who practiced yoga. Her clientele, whoever they turned out to be, would not live in this neighbourhood.

People will travel some distance these days. They'll come on bicycles, she predicted.

The floors are of polished birch. Heavy industrial sewing machines, once bolted to the boards, left holes. Two young women, new to carpentry, worked around them as they did the refinishing. Ydessa pointed to pockmarks, gouges, scrapes, besides the bolt holes. Leave them, she said, much to their surprise.

She formulates a connection that gives her pleasure. Her practices reveal the beauty of old tensions.

Early every morning she moves alone through her yoga sequences on a mat on the studio floor, drawing slow appreciation from the marks and gaps of her own occupation, marks that reveal faint pulsations, which, on a good day, she can release through attention and breath. Sometimes she meditates on the history of gouges and pockmarks, whole sets of conditions pulsing there. The senses are horses, gouges and pockmarks what they range over. The mind is reins. The rider she has become holds firm the mind, leaps over the fear-inducing gaps of every day.

In a clean level place, free from pebbles, fire, and gravel, by the sound of water and other desiderata favourable to thought, inoffensive to the eye, in a hidden retreat protected from the wind, there one should practice yoga, she read in the *Svetasvatara Upanishad*.

She calls her studio Spirit Level.

By closing the ears with our thumbs, we hear the space within the heart. Of this space there is a sevenfold equivalent: like a river, a bell, a brass vessel, a wheel, the croaking of frogs, rain, or when one speaks in a sheltered place. She instructs her students to place their thumbs firmly in their ears.

Notions held by each student, ranging from tense refusal to willing and arduous effort, are energies that pulse across the bright floor. Relinquishment is hers alone. They sit together, cross-legged in the luminous room, thumbs firmly pressing ears, breathing becoming more regular, deeper, their minds roaming as thoughts are observed, dispensed with, scattered then gathered into observation once more. The very same obstacles encountered by beginners for thousands of years are here with them in the room — sloth, ennui, hunger, craving, pride, shame, the compulsions. Though no one speaks, the room is full of craning effort to formulate in words the new happiness each hopes to discover.

This is her happiness. She feels it as a privilege and a blessing: seven students trying something.

Henry is coming.

The thought presses its nose to a window. It vanishes. The point of contact retains heat, brief, fleeting. The glass cools.

Here are the conditions of her life in Toronto: a storefront studio, above it a small apartment with bed, table, and chair. A bicycle, stored in the stairwell, is her chief mode of transportation, no matter the weather.

Of her students she asks ten dollars per class. In a good month she earns two thousand dollars. With this revenue she pays her mortgage ($700), covers her insurance ($300), her utilities ($200), purchases food and other necessities. She gives the remainder away. Her investment values rise and fall. Six million. Seven.

She buys her yoga wear and street clothing — T-shirts and stretch pants and simple dresses — at proliferating thrift shops, where she has begun to notice an abundance of never-before-worn items. Her students outfit themselves in expensive yoga gear from new businesses flourishing in the sudden craze for yoga.

They inquire about mats and bolsters and lavender-filled eye pillows, having seen these items for sale at larger studios. For floor mats she encourages her students to shop at Canadian Tire. And what about the other items? She loses one or two students each week to the larger studios, to teachers who sell yoga accessories and are closer to the students' places of work, who offer teacher training and remain faithful to year-long class schedules by hiring substitute teachers when owners take time off. Some students want a website with monthly updates, or music played during the hour-and-a-half sessions, familiar music, music heard elsewhere, or they want aerobic-paced classes, want to sweat in a crowded studio. Some want men.

She rarely sees a man at her studio.

There was one who attended classes for about half a year. The spirit level is a carpentry tool, he said.

Yes, it is.

Do you think you are constructing something here?

His hostility was direct and spontaneous but quickly withdrawn. He clasped her hand. She didn't see him again.

Shortly after September 11, 2001, a student turned up asking unusual questions. Does the body hold its pain in energy cysts, and, if so, why? At fifty years of age could she truly hope for significant change in her ways of approaching life? How did Ydessa manage her spiritual quest while living in the mundane world? Why had she left her safe haven of peace at the ashram to re-enter the mess of the everyday? Though the questions were serious and stark, the student had a glorious sense of humour, and Ydessa was happy to answer as well and as fully as she could. Now, after two years of regular practice, this woman enters class with a slight bow, arranges her mat carefully, speaks to no one. She removes the one ring she wears, assumes the forward bend, breathing deeply in *Ujjahi*, and sits cross-legged, patiently awaiting instruction. Her white hair is cut short, she wears loose white cotton pants and a white T-shirt.

I have ruptured the plane, she tells Ydessa. She says little more.

They sit together, students and instructor, in the luminous room, all cross-legged, thumbs pressed in their ears. In the streets a car horn blares, somewhere an apartment dweller begins to sing along to a Billie Holliday recording, *Them that's got shall get, them that's not shall lose / So the Bible says, and it still is news*, each of them more or less aware of the worldly sounds. It is seven o'clock on a Wednesday evening, May 2003. On the other side of town, walking head down in the direction of Spirit Level, comes Henry Rattle.

THREE

HE ARRIVED IN Toronto by train and took the subway to the corner of Spadina and Bloor. That evening he went out alone to a West End sports bar where he consumed three pints of beer in two hours, sitting on a stool, watching hockey in the amicable company of twelve young men. Occasionally someone uttered a quick shout, occasionally a collective groan rose in the air. When the game was over he walked back to his friend's house, not one sustained thought in his head.

What was that thing moving slowly at the foot of the driveway? He had to squint to make it out. A raccoon, lying on its side. Closer, he saw there was blood at its anus.

He crouched beside the wounded animal. Go easy, he said.

No light blazed in the house, Tyler not yet home from night class. What to do? The creature's eyes rolled in their sockets, wet, frightened.

Henry's stomach lurched.

Listen, I'm going to call someone. He had a house key. Who to call? He didn't know.

I'll be right back. Go easy.

The woman who answered the phone at animal rescue asked him if the animal were dying. Is it able to get up? What I mean is, would it be likely to move off before we can get there? You should put something over it. Cover it to keep it from leaving.

He thought he could remember a small blanket on an upper shelf in the hall closet.

She said, Maybe a box. A recycling box would be excellent.

Oh. A recycling box. He thought she'd meant something to give the raccoon comfort. No. This was business.

When he returned to the drive the raccoon was lying on its back, panting, its long black claws retracted, its glistening eyes blinking slowly.

I'm trying to think! he shouted.

He found a blue recycling box at the side of the house, and a short stick that branched like a slingshot. He propped the box over the raccoon, making it a cubbyhole, a little air circulating, some dim light. But now their gaze was severed. Now he had to stand apart. Henry's heart filled with sadness. After a while he went back into the house.

In the early morning he finds the box overturned, the raccoon gone, and no message from animal rescue to say if they had taken it away. I should have stayed, he thinks, I should have stayed with it, I should never have covered it with that fucking box.

He walks westward along College, thinking of the raccoon's lambent eyes. *Beseeching* is the word he settles on. No, *imploring*. He had heard a mind cry out, had tried to respond. What does not let go is the image of that blue box placed over the raccoon, blocking its gaze, reducing what had passed between them to a mere commotion. Maybe the raccoon had seen his feet. It's almost pornographic, he is thinking, to deprive a dying creature of sight. Unforgivable. I should have stayed with it. I should have sat down next to it, though its eyes were rolling, its legs stiffening and claws retracting, belly exposed. Fuck it. I should have stayed till its last moment alive.

Within this lamentation he is nauseous. He thinks of the term *roadkill*, of the formless, faceless, ageless, genderless agent that lies within the term. Even the vehicle is missing. Only the road and what the road destroys. The world is full of things indifferent to life, even hostile. He had tried not to be among them. He observes College Street, the night air filling with scents from spring gardens. Automobiles lining both lanes of traffic, curb spaces jammed, the street's activities capably overwhelming the senses of every individual passing through. It's a carnival, just as it's intended to be. He is walking in argument toward Ydessa Bloom.

FOUR

ONCE THERE WAS a time when Henry's father walked the honey lines like a man dancing. Then Henry's mother died and his father's feet danced no longer. Nothing during Henry's late childhood, nothing during his adolescence, had ever induced his father to move again as he had when his wife lived. The lines of his father's movements, which Henry recorded in small ink drawings, became straight, short, repetitive: there and back, there and back, without music. Now his father is dead, and he is walking toward Ydessa. Twenty-four years old. How did your father die? Ydessa will ask him later, drinking wine with him, but carefully, at a small table in an almost empty bar. They will have been together two hours before she asks him that. And he will answer that his father hung himself. About that he will say no more.

She is ascending a flight of stairs in a house of dreams. She knows how to navigate its rotting steps, knows to allow shadows to pulse forward, knows how to enter spaces between particle and wave, knows to look for what is carried between the spaces. The colourful days are swinging round again. When she thought of Henry over the years — when she conjured moving pictures of him — he had language, an entire arsenal of words. She will never forget the morning he admitted to finding Roger's arm. He called her a drinking person that day. This dim bar, with its ruddy gold light, this mute young man. She had not anticipated such silence. She watches him flex the muscles in his beautiful arms, wordless. He hunches over the table, his wine glass almost obscured.

She asks where he is staying, and for how long. He tells her he is sleeping on his friend Tyler's couch.

Is it comfortable there?

Henry shrugs. It's all right.

You can stay with me, if you like. I have room. The place is very simple. No TV, no radio. Eleven shades of white and not much more. But. You're welcome.

The look on his face is of astonishment. Diffuse light falls across his eyes.

You hardly know me.

These words surprise her. But she keeps her face neutral. My memory is binding, she replies. I think I know everything I need to know.

———

Would you like to stay with me, Henry?

I am so broken, he says into the glass of wine tipped to his mouth. Not a welcome houseguest. No, he doesn't utter these words. She gives other words to him, placing them gently in his mouth. What he says, returning his glass to the table, is, All right.

Someone has chosen from the jukebox playlist Renata Scotto's "Un bel di vedremo" from *Madame Butterfly*.

Madame Butterfly, Ydessa says.

Henry's face is lowered.

One fine day we'll see a wisp of smoke rising over the furthest edge of the sea. And then the ship appears. I don't go down to meet him.

She waits but he does not speak.

You are very beautiful, she tells him, and he lifts his face, dumbfounded. The spit of your father when he was your age.

In the story of Madame Butterfly — but maybe you know it?

He shakes his head.

In the story, a young US naval officer marries a very young Japanese woman. He gets her with child then leaves her. She waits for him, but he isn't true. Such a common story. Friendship fails, love is bankrupt. Do you know very much about this?

Not too much.

Have you been in love?

The light in his eyes flickers. Though Renata Scotto's voice is soaring, he doesn't respond to the rising emotion.

I remember how you used to draw the patterns of the world. Do you still carry a fountain pen and a little sketchbook?

He reaches into his back pocket, produces a small black notebook, which he places carefully on the table, reaches for his pen.

I try to draw, he mumbles. I gave it up for years and then recently I took it up again. I can't afford a fountain pen.

And?

The pages aren't large enough for —. He tries again. Anyway, he says, timid, agitated, it's too late. Drawing, it turns out, is destructive.

Destructive? Really? How so?

He lays his beautiful head down on the table, groaning a little. Too inhibiting. It turns off the sounds around me. I want those sounds.

She reaches across the table, takes his hand. He raises his head a little. She smiles.

It isn't like you to be defeatist. It wasn't.

She releases his hand, lifts her glass. She takes a small sip, observing him over the rim. The violence of him.

The world is not against us, you know.

Their server returns. Care for another round?

I'll have a soda water. Henry?

Okay.

The server turns to Ydessa.

I'm Whitney. I'm in your Tuesday and Thursday night classes. What? I'm sorry. . .

Whitney is looking at Henry. He is straightening, pulling his shoulders back and down, opening his countenance, revealing himself a little. He attempts something close to a smile. Whitney's smile is broad.

This is my friend Henry. Ydessa places her hand lightly on his forearm. We haven't seen each other in years.

Do you practice yoga, Henry?

No.

You should take a class with Ydessa. It's transcendental.

Beneath the flimsy strap of Whitney's sheer dress, the figure of Tantalus hangs from the bough of a fruit tree laden with pears and figs and pomegranates. Food for the dead. The work of a skilled tattoo artist.

Ydessa's truly awesome, Whitney says. She gives us our space, lets us fall apart without interference. She's strong as an ox. She places her hand lightly on Henry's shoulder as she leaves their table.

Ydessa excuses herself.

Graffiti on the wall of the washroom cubicle says *I fucked your mother*.

Go home, Dad, you're drunk, someone has scribbled below.

That girl wants to seduce Henry and he is already falling for it, magnetized. A nearly naked, saucy, tattooed warrior of the twenty-first century, this Whitney. Strike a pose. What do her students imagine when she introduces Warrior Pose? What did this young woman with Tantalus hanging on her back make of *Virabhadrasana*?

Something hostile in young city women. *I fucked your mother.* You and the whole world, sweetheart, she says aloud.

She's washing her hands in the ultramodern chrome sink. She didn't manage grace in her young life, no, not at all, but still she wants to say to the young ones — what? Love yourself and this planet, don't fuck it up. Preposterous. In this tiny bar on Dundas Street, something hostile. She can sense it.

On her left pinkie she wears a silver band engraved with the words *I remember I forget*. Once a very thin boy, Henry is thin yet, reticent, and astonishingly beautiful. Absolutely beautiful, a tunnel of light.

How has he become the inert creature sitting with her now? Where had he learned to dress his life so plainly? She stretches out her hands to touch the mirror. They reach back, catching her sudden surprising sorrow.

Coming out of the washroom she sees Henry from a completely different angle. He is drumming his fingers on the cover of his small notebook. His hair is falling into his eyes, he flips it back. She stops, dazzled, puts her hand to her mouth. He is unaware of his movements. His hair falls again over his eyes. As he flips it a second time he notices her at the door of the women's washroom. She offers him a shy smile.

As she sits, she asks, And how is your father, Henry?

Did you ever see Teresa again?

Someone at the jukebox selects a song that causes wild laughter to lift from the corner of the room. He turns to observe those laughing. Some emotion twists and sags in the otherwise firm flesh of his face. His breath is very short, travelling high in his chest. He turns back to Ydessa.

Did you see Teresa? She had breast cancer. Her left breast was removed. Did you know about this?

She nods.

The April after you and your father moved to Picton, I went back to Baptiste, stayed with Barri for a while. I wanted to see you, but the timing was never right. While I was there I made a few decisions and talked them over with Barri. She disapproved of my plan to go to the yoga centre.

Henry is watching the young people in the corner. What did she think you should have done instead? he asks.

Gone alone into the woods to read for five years.

He laughs, turning back to see if she is joking. You weren't a reader. What made her say that?

She allows his tone, his pitch, to enter her. After a while, she says, Barri was quoting a famous teacher, Joseph Campbell.

I've heard of that guy. His work influenced *Star Wars*.

Barri knew how to grind a large question down to manageable size. Go to the woods was a kind of brilliant metaphor. I went to the ashram in 1989, I came out in 1999, and for many of those years I was asking myself, Could I go to the woods now? How about now?

On your own in an ashram for ten years seems like the woods to me.

———

They are walking close in the soft night air. He has agreed to walk to her studio, but he won't stay with her, will continue to sleep on his friend's couch, will return to her once he secures a job, when he's more independent. Tonight she'll give him a key.

They climb the stairs to her small apartment above the studio. Just as she has described it, a monk's cell in shades of white, a bed, a table, a chair. Refinished birch floors that shine. Plain white cotton blinds over the windows, a rattan room divider. You could be quite modest behind that Japanese screen, she jokes. No television, no computer, at least only in the studio. You're welcome to use it when the studio is closed. The apartment is one large room, kitchen at one end, bathroom down a hall, which students share. Walls unadorned, embellishments absent. One bed.

Did she mean for them to sleep together? he wonders.

I will surely disturb you if I stay here.

Not at all, she answers swiftly. Of course, it's up to you. But I'd enjoy your company.

If you're sure. His breath is very short and very high.

The sparsity of her place frightens him. It disturbs his own barrenness. Modern things in general frighten him, but this almost total absence of things strikes him as perverse. The Ydessa he remembers was in love with shiny things. That Ydessa was fast, loaded, edgy. Walking along College Street earlier in the evening, he had imagined her as she had been — what? Foxy. Yes, foxy: flashy. But she is austere now, he thinks. How can this be? He finds her alarming. She is nothing and also everything he remembers.

She gives him a key while explaining tomorrow's teaching

schedule, then bids him good night. She places her hands on his upper arms and kisses first one and then the other cheek. Good night, Henry.

Her smile is wide. She is gorgeous, as beautiful as he has ever known any woman to be.

Henry was the one who found his father, the one who lifted his father's limp body while he struggled with one hand to remove the rope from his neck. He staggered on the chair under the weight released. He carried his father into the farmhouse to lay him down on the living room sofa. He can't ask Ydessa did she ever go to the woods to read, because the where escapes him. She means the woods symbolically, but where in the world are they? What of the world worth measuring could steady the ground that is forever slipping from under one's feet?

His deep and abiding ignorance, the animal he has become.

He takes a job at a bar on College Street, a place Whitney recommends. She's friendly with the owner, works at another place owned by the same man. During evenings when Henry works and Whitney is off for the night, she cycles over and sits on a stool at his bar, nursing a vodka tonic, waiting for him to be through. They go back to her place, talking seldom if at all. They fuck, vacantly, and their fucking is a contractual agreement between two bodies: ten minutes to one orgasm, five to the other. He doesn't give her what she wants, and she doesn't ask. He tells her not to speak about him with Ydessa, and she doesn't. When he thinks of Ydessa instructing students in the myriad yoga poses, as Teresa once instructed Ydessa, he turns cold. Locked in.

Thought has no quality in common with the physical world, except intensity, which in mathematical terms can be considered frequency. What are Henry's thoughts on such a mathematical scale during the ninety days he stays silent and apart from Ydessa, never calling to explain, leaving her to wonder what happened to him. How quick are his thoughts relative to normal thinking, to normal thought frequency or intensity? Time can come to a standstill when the flow of energy is this intense.

For ninety days he stays away. The summer drains. Shame runs up and down his spine. Fruitlessly employed, aimless, his mind moving at high speeds while his body ossifies, he can't stay with her in that small, holy place, not while he is an animal in a fit of dislocation. He is not to be observed, not by her.

FIVE

HE FINGERS THE key to Ydessa's apartment, like a worry stone kept in his pocket. He knows he should go to her. He remembers her at Baptiste as high voltage, almost fire. But now she has settled. He doesn't know how to act in the company of such a slow and considerate woman who loves him. He hates the serenity manifest in her.

He has ruined every relationship he has ever had. He is thoroughly flawed. He walks in the direction of her studio, on a beautiful afternoon in August such as poets might try, and fail, to write about, incommensurable and inscrutable, sunlight sprightly, flashing in windows of shops and restaurants. College Street sounds are bright, distinct. The air is warm, a slight breeze slides over his skin. The windows of the street are open, everyone is looking in, out, everyone is young, alive. Young men are shouting at television sets suspended above bottles of whisky, multiplied in wall mirrors. Aware of themselves. Nothing like Picton, he thinks. Does he admire the muscular city or does it seem too full of itself? Two young women ahead of him are walking like cats with tails up, sex and disdain intermingled. He shouldn't be signalling the slightest interest in Whitney. Her high hopes, her dependency, the way she demands his attention. He is hopeless. No one should put any hope in him.

Ydessa is wearing a cream-coloured linen shift, her arms and legs bare. She strikes an attitude both relaxed and alert. Hello, old friend, she says. She seems genuinely happy to see him, says nothing about his absence. She invites him in, but when he says, No, let's go for a drink at the Communist's Daughter, she accepts without hesitation.

I'll get some money.

No. My treat this time. I've been working. Just get your shoes.

Two lone customers, a man and a woman, look up as Henry and Ydessa enter the bar. The woman is large and slovenly. Her head is shaved.

The Daughter herself, Ydessa whispers, bowing slightly in the woman's direction.

Henry's fingers twitch. He shoves them into his pockets.

She comes to yoga classes. She's resilient for a woman her size and age, and very funny. She told me she carries the failure of communism in a cyst in her left hip.

Henry snorts. Do you believe all that?

All what?

This New Age bullshit. Talk about memories residing in bone and muscle.

Ydessa catches the waitress's eye and gestures toward their table. I don't think of it as bullshit. New Age is just a label for a different kind of thinking. You don't have to buy it wholesale.

You should slap your students down when they say stuff like that.

That's not my way. I'm not that kind of teacher.

The waitress comes and takes their order. Her eyes settle for an instant on Henry's upturned face.

I find it curious, Ydessa says, that old people can have sudden vivid recollections of childhood events. The colour of a mother's dressing gown, its rather peculiar shade of blue. The way an uncle shifted his weight, standing uncomfortably at a summer picnic, strawberries sliding dangerously on his plate. Maybe synapses are much more than gaps. Maybe the old spaces leak memory as they weaken. Or maybe we are less tense in later years, we allow more things to enter. Well. A quick conclusion is always irresistible, isn't it.

The waitress reappears. Henry takes a sip of his beer. He picks up Ydessa's hand.

We lost my mother's ring.

The lights in the bar go out, the thrum of its motors cease.

Shah mat, Ydessa says. The king is helpless.

What? He doesn't understand, but he is oblivious to the cessation of light and hum in the room. He says again, My mother's ring.

She leans toward him, seizes his upper arms, feels his blood receive her. He tenses, stiffens.

Let's go back to my place. She is rising.

But we've just got our drinks.

Come on.

He digs into his front pocket, finds a crumpled twenty, unfolds and irons it flat between his palms.

Best to leave the money on the table. You'll have to leave all of it. Their cash register is useless now.

He doesn't understand her. When he stands, it is to follow her. He can't conceive why he holds to her will as to a rope. He lays the twenty down.

A streetcar sits idle on the Dundas Street tracks, impatient faces pressed against the windows. Traffic lights are out, traffic at a standstill. A young man in a Cat in the Hat T-shirt is directing drivers around the stopped streetcar. Ydessa takes Henry's hand.

People have come out of shops and houses to ask what is happening. A shaft of late afternoon sun flares across a gap between two low buildings, a meteor of light across his eyes as he at last catches her meaning.

The king is helpless. A trick of surrender.

S I X

IN HIS DREAM a child asks, Why does each person need five stones? On waking he watches Ydessa moving in candlelight, her skin incandescent. He rises out of the tangled sheets, finds his jeans, removes notebook and pen from a back pocket, and begins to draw her. The question of five stones lingers heavily in his moving hand.

You have struck a heroic attitude, she says after observing him for a while as he sits on the side of her bed, sketching naked in candlelight. He hears her vaguely, remotely. He disappears into the drawing, remembering this safety after long absence, the safety and the soft pressure of his hand, his notebook where it rests on his naked thigh.

He is tumescent: she sees and reacts with a second hunger.

She had lifted her dress above her head, shown no reaction to his sharp ingress of breath behind her. It was the strength of her, the certainty, her contained vitality, the assuredness in the long muscles of her thighs, the rounded muscles of her ass, which had surprised him, these and the absence of undergarments. He had realized instantly that the Ydessa of his first knowing, she of Baptiste Lake, the thirty-year-old Ydessa, had gone around half naked then as well. He came toward her from behind, cupping her small breasts in his hands. He pressed himself into her, but she turned around and looked at him, touching herself between her legs. He took her to the bed, and she allowed him to come into her, quickly. Her cry was short, her breath so thin. Now he is drawing her portrait, his steady hand holding the heat of her. She lifts into a handstand, all grace, looking through the inverted room at an inverted Henry and his crooked smile.

You have all my attention, he says, ceasing to draw

She laughs. I had it before.

But now, in all seriousness. She drops to the floor. We must go out. Or I must go. I have to walk up to my parents' place. My mother will be frightened.

I'll come with you. Turning away from his drawing, rising, gathering his clothes. When he turns toward her she is once again lifting her arms above her head to drop the linen dress over her astonishing body. He goes to her and presses his palm against her pubis. The muscles in her thighs tense, animated then softened.

Ydessa.

She laughs. Henry.

The streets are full of human voices singing and laughing in the dark. An unusual pressure is being exerted, they feel it, a sweet and gentle exertion flowing over their skin. Human joy is beating in the street, a current of banging and thumping. Overhead: three thousand stars. Someone has set up a table at the corner of Dundas and Ossington and placed a hurricane lamp on it. Encircled within the lamp's golden light are four large ice cream tubs, and, next to these, plastic cups and plastic spoons.

Eat me. Ydessa laughs easily. Henry's happiness intensifies. They fill two cups.

This night is so unbelievable. Henry is stretching his arm around Ydessa's waist to bring her close. She spins in to kiss his soft mouth then spins away again beyond his hold, turning a pirouette.

Draw that! she commands, holding her plastic cup high. You bogus artist!

Ydessa. He can't help saying her name out loud.

In the darkness of her apartment she had been luminous, he ardent. He had walked toward her a broken man. Now his heart feels doubled, a new equation. Henry and Ydessa: lovers. Unbelievable, and it stops him in his tracks. Might there be a pattern here that he could get down on paper? Might a welcome adjustment materialize out of the stifling irregularity of his days?

Ydessa?

Yes?

Will you take another ice cream?

Yes, Love, I believe I will.

Love.

The quaintness of Henry's manner amuses a woman who arrives with him at the makeshift table. She laughs. Carpe diem, is that it? Eh? At my melting roadside buffet, ladies and gentlemen! *Senhoras e senhores!* Seize the night!

She dishes up two cups of velvety chocolate ice cream.

What is your name, Philosopher? Let me always remember

you, the loveliest moment of this *louco* night.

Henry Rattle.

Would you say he is a marvel? Ydessa rises into a handstand, her brown legs straight like tapers, her shift dropping to her hips.

Ydessa!

Hosanna!

She drops down to the pavement, bows slightly and receives the proffered cup of ice cream. The woman laughs.

Magnificent! One can be without shame in the dark. No underpants, why not? In the dark the eyes are gone. What a night. I haven't enjoyed myself so much in years.

Spaciousness flares in Henry's heart.

They make their way north on Bathurst Street. The night carries the strong smell of barbecued meat, the sound of laughter.

Listen, Ydessa, they're singing.

Yes. They're happy.

I'm happy.

Shine on, Sweetheart.

Rose and Sam are sitting in the dark living room, Rose's hands clutched in her lap. A small red candle is burning on the table between them. Her eyes are closed.

From his chair, her father smiles weakly as she ushers Henry into the room.

Poppa. We've come to see how you are making out.

Nothing much making, he says, tilting his head in Rose's direction.

Were you at supper when the power went out?

It happened before. They came to the door, told us we should come down in any case. Cold supper. Cold cuts.

Aha, a change of menu. They were originally planning hot cuts.

Now her father's smile is full. Ydessala.

And Rose?

As you see.

Nothing more than what I see?

No.

All the angles in her father's thin face are curving, flowing. He is relieved to see her.

Henry, these are my parents. Rose and Samuel Bloom, meet Henry Rattle.

Rose takes hold of her cheeks and squeezes her face but does not open her eyes. You are Ydessa's student?

No. Yes.

A decisive man you've brought to us on this night of darkness, Ydessala.

Perhaps a little indecisive, yes, but Momma, he's gorgeous.

Rose peers out between slits her eyelids make. I'll give you this, she says after a while.

Would you like to take a walk? The streets are very interesting.

The streets are interesting. What are they doing, these interesting streets?

They're giving food away. They're dancing, laughing. They're making love.

For this they need no lights?

Right. For this they need a power outage.

Tomorrow all the women will be pregnant.

Right. And all the ice cream will be liquid.

Ice cream I eat tonight will *make* liquid.

Sam says, Some things don't change, Rose, even when the lights go out.

Ydessa says, C'mon, Momma, come out for a bit. The sky is a work of art.

This gorgeous boy will come too?

If you like. You can hold his hand.

Where do your parents live, Henry Rattle?

My parents are both dead, Mrs. Bloom.

Oy gevalt. To be so young without parents.

She urges them again to get up from their chairs. Come on. Let's go out. Such a night. Let's walk eight blocks and be changed forever. That's not such a commitment, really, for the promise?

Ydessala, Sam says, what's come over you? You are irrepressible.

You have never seen such stars in Toronto, Poppa, I promise you. Thousands of streetlights have flown into the sky.

Streetlights in the sky! Well, Rose? What do you say?

All right, get my wrap. If Ydessala is irrepressible tonight, something to see must be believed.

Sam kisses Rose lightly on her damp forehead. I'll bring your shawl from the bedroom. She can catch cold from a warm summer breeze even. We'll take some precautions, I think, despite the promised transfiguration.

———

In lockstep they venture out along the street, Rose in back with Henry, his arm steadying her, Ydessa and Sam leading the way, without destination, trading the impulse each feels, to veer left or right, a little machine of forward movement and faith. Three thousand stars, all of them visible.

Look, Momma: the glorious beauty of the sky.

I've seen the sky before. Show me something new.

Together they angle past another tight-knit foursome moving in the opposite direction down Bathurst Street. The man in front is playing a clarinet, the stick held high in his hands. He is swaying side to side. The woman stops to address Ydessa.

Oh wow! My yoga instructor in a power failure! Karmic.

Y is for yoga and Ydessala! Rose sings out, surprising herself, and claps her hand over her mouth. Sam laughs, catching the spirit of Rose's hijinks.

I is for the night has a thousand eyes.

Ydessa groans softly, jabs Sam in the ribs. *Oomph*. He is playful, his fist in her face. *You*.

The musician raises his instrument to the sky, and blows.

You're like a man with twenty fingers, she says as if to no one.

Well, are we spelling something here, or not? Sam asks.

D is for the dark. Delirious. *Dummkopf*.

Such impertinence!

Reb Yid!

Look up there, Rose cries. Someone waving the sparklers!

She moves away from the little group, and Sam falls back to be with her. Ydessa pulls Henry toward her and kisses him.

Happy new year, he whispers. He speaks awkwardly, catching her hand, pulling her back, his tongue sweet and brief in her mouth. Wild music drifts down the escarpment.

———

Are you frightened, Rose?

No. Thieves will be downtown or in the suburbs. As you see, it is almost all goodwill on these interesting streets.

You are changed forever, as Ydessa promised?

Such a long time since humanity has impressed me. Oh, such a long time.

Forget that thought, Rose. Stay here in this bright sparkle. Your face looks so lovely.

My father is a romantic, Ydessa explains to Henry. Pretty soon he'll be crooning Frank Sinatra.

What will he sing?

"Fly Me to the Moon."

And let me sail among the stars. In other words, please be true.

You know this song?

Please be true: my mother and father used to dance to this song.

She places her hand lightly on his arm. He looks at her and observes the fox. Observes also, below the fox, another animal, one he wants.

What are you? he whispers. Tell me what you are. He places his hand on her breast.

No, she hisses, stepping back. This is not for my parents to know.

You're ashamed?

No. My mother —

She will say no more.

But Rose has seen Henry's hand on her daughter's breast and the pain lifts up. She sighs deeply.

I will go home now. Sam, take me home. Do not worry about us. Have fun, Ydessa, with this handsome young man half your age. We were already finished with transformation anyway.

She grips her shawl, pulls it tight to her small rounded shoulders. She has closed her eyes.

Sam's quick appeal to Ydessa, an ancient one, goes unacknowledged.

Though it is almost impossible to detect shadow in this dark place on this black night, Henry feels a large, dense, wordlessness descend. He waits for Ydessa to indicate what should be done next, and she does not. Instead she moves ahead, alone and unimpeded, through the intersection that has brought bewilderment and uncertainty back to him. She moves as a wheel on fire. Where a moment ago there was harmony, his mistake has thrown him out of gear. The moment is lost. What is it? What has happened? There is shame everywhere he looks.

From out of the hollow comes a flash of his father's lost waltz, the sad gait he kept across the fields in Prince Edward County, an impenetrable stony solitaire, moving within himself at a discordant pace.

I want to know —, Henry begins. But he is silenced by her sudden step toward Sam, whom she embraces. Advancing to her mother, she kisses Rose, lightly, on both cheeks.

If the power is out in the morning, I won't be able to open the studio. I'll come up, with coffee if I can find any.

We don't need you to come up.

She kisses Rose's forehead. But even so, I might see you tomorrow morning.

Sam steps forward and puts his arm around Rose's shoulders. Say good night.

He turns to Henry. You'll come visit us another time.

A crown of living sparks shoots round his head, behind him a small face is briefly illuminated in the showering light of a sparkler as a child writes her name in the night.

I cursed them for their cheerful ignorance, I cursed them for their refusal to look deeply into things. For their neglect. I suppose Rose curses me for abandoning her. I could not follow her, obviously. She would have kept me by her side through all our days. To see me making eyes at a man I will not marry is to shake my fist at her laws.

Henry stops. Are you already leaving me?

Oh Henry.

I mean it. Why are limits being set?

It is not me who is setting limits. Can you imagine our suffering were we to insist on trying to stay together? It's far too soon for this conversation, Love.

———

They are walking in the middle of the road, passing through inter-section after intersection. Occasionally, and then increasingly, as they walk south, in passing windows Henry sees the small flickering flames of tapered candles, flames of ruddy gold. Individuals try-ing to live out the blackout in soft romance. He is subject to a growing feeling that the candles are accusations rife with meaning, accompanying him in a now formal procession, a condemned man approaching the hanging tree. Ydessa is quiet. He has offended her, and why — now, in his worry and fear — does he feel his cock flex and lift, his longing sudden and sharp? Ridiculous. She won't have him again.

But there is only her to think of in this slow walk toward the lake, Ydessa in unseemly quietude, her hips rolling in the heat of the night. They have been sexual, more than once she has called him Love, but now there is nothing. His hands are futile, his body a nuisance, or, worse, an enemy. He could take her right here in the street.

His happiness circles the drain and is gone. Now there is only dense shadow in these bleak and silent streets.

All across the eastern seaboard, overburdened transmission lines sagged till they touched the trees below and shorted out. This was the night, had they known how to imagine it, that a satellite camera captured the state of the world: broken connections, disabled power, defeat of energy.

He is not strong enough for Ydessa.

At midday many traffic lights are still not working. Cars creep along, drivers strangely accommodating, gesturing to one another, please go first. The irony of the accommodation is not lost on Henry, as he travels by slow taxi away from her. Something about the sapphire. Surely Ydessa thinks less of him. They had fucked a second time, a third, she had allowed it. They had slept. He had accepted a cup of coffee, had turned away from her at the door and wouldn't look back even when she called out. His arrival had been at first completely absorbing, but surely now her interest in him is lost. His littleness is pathetic. He is destroying everything.

Whitney. She will be impossible. He is scheduled to work an afternoon shift and is travelling away from the obligation. He'll go back to the county. Neither Whitney nor Ydessa will know how to find him. He'll close his father's life, clear the house, yes, sell his father's few effects.

Sick buoyancy fills the bowl of his solar plexus. He can go somewhere: out west. California. He can disappear into the mountains, he can work for a beekeeper in some valley. He can leave this fucking mess. He can disappear. He can forget that either woman ever saw him naked.

He stands in line in the bus terminal, affecting a determination he does not feel.

SEVEN

AT THE ASHRAM no sex was allowed between single participants. Married residents had permission to engage in moderate sexual activity. Disciplined, rigorous, scheduled meditation and dream analysis were the ways to defeat the craving instincts.

Most people who meditate aren't meditating, Rass told her. Most people who try meditation are too attached to pleasure to enter fully into the practice. But if you can enter into it, even for a second, you begin to see how distracted you are. Very soon you begin to understand how distracted everyone is. You thought you could leave all that has happened behind? No, there it is, sheltering in your distraction. And then you feel that your circulating blood and your nerves are fully exposed, that you are skinless, unmediated.

For five years, to labour in the ways demanded by the guru, she woke every morning at four. On the first morning of her sixth year he came to her to explain the new strategy: she would be his lover, the *is* that would now *be*. Her time had come to enter the realm of the innermost sanctum, he said, his smile a command. Our carnal bodies, our animal selves, our two energies will enter an orbit and a harmony, and like the heavenly bodies that kiss in their passing, I will come to you every twenty-eight days; you must keep a schedule and ready yourself for me. We will pass the hours like Venus and Ceres in the star-strewn sky, our ultraslow congress like starlight bringing harmony to the planet in the years to come. Now, Ydessa, remove your robe.

Dogs ran in her then, dogs and runaway horses. She could say nothing. In complete silence she stood before him, holding tight to the collar of her robe, while his face, which hid nothing, shot into rage at her non-acquiescence, her immense inadequacy. You will do as I say, he shouted, and she would not, would say nothing. The horses ran, their hooves pounding, roiling the dust, running as a many-legged beast, jagged, panicked, bolting through circuits of blood with the fury of an electrical fire, while the guru's extravagant face filled with ire, disbelief, then loathing. How he despised her.

You have learned nothing, he hissed. You are grasping, your vision just as impure as when you first arrived. As if to destroy her with his immense authority, he shouted, Leave my sight.

You are a yoga teacher. You have made vows. Henry cannot change these things. Sex with Henry, the memories pouring forth from all the years, cannot change these things. Energy gathers, is dammed up, is denied. Frustrated, it's stoppered. Energy releases, victorious — life goes on amid the ceaseless, swirling cascade.

Power is restored, the lights in the studio come on. She had been on the verge of tears as the day gathered its energy, slowly moving her into clarity, and now her body, which had been flowing, is suddenly checked. Cut.

She bows to nobody.
Namaste.

An old woman died last night. Sam is leading her into the suite as he whispers what he knows. They found her on the floor. She had unplugged the lamp cord from the wall socket. She was stretching for the outlet, had lowered to her knees, rocked onto her hip, and turned over onto her belly. You can imagine this ninety-year-old. The authorities say she was trying to regain the light, not realizing that the whole city was in darkness.

If only I could say this less clearly, Ydessa. She was reaching for the light. I wish to God your mother would make the same effort, just once.

She tires of repeating phrases and names of pose flows, tires of old tales about the long journey, its diversions and unexpected interruptions, the caution — be prepared for sudden crossroads. The journey is easily thrown. Fine balance is required. She tells her students they will long for direction from a teacher or guide, but then the longing will pass. Do not pin longing on any place, any map, or any one.

Wonder glorious and wonder wretched. Who at Baptiste relinquished his son for a blind hive, which he took up like a shield that was his stolen life, awful indignity. Who took a plain summer with its secrets sweetening the air and turned it sweeter. What neighbour honour mother father wastrel mathematician whose heart, bleak, breaks, and harder yet the breakthrough, heart a desert while another floods and teems. Whose tracks were followed, whose lost, whose beauty first and what lasts. Who was the eternal child, who the one who could not help but die.

Her breath and her thoughts are all. She can unify the breath with her movement. She reaches around the core of her body, twisting in *Ardha Matsendrasana*, reaching for the back wall, which could be a projection on a screen flickering in light and shadow. Here is the beauty of Henry, the holy moment, the terrible defilement. His cock had been harder than she remembered possible. As she came each time on the night of the blackout, as the low sounds in her throat began to grow, expanding, Roger, he who had been gone for years, placed his hand on her head. Afterwards Henry lay outstretched beside her, his body slick and glistening. He placed his index finger inside her mouth and she closed her lips and held it there, tenderly.

They are arguing, have been arguing for many hours. He is possessed by a question. Over and over he tells himself not to ask this question, and then he asks: Will we be lovers again?

In the swirling darkness he cannot see her clearly.

Let's let what wants to come, come. Praise the Brahman, praise the cow, praise the dog, and the eaters of dog.

I want to know, Ydessa.

She takes his hand.

How can I know if we will be lovers again? The work of years has been to disrupt the idea that the future is knowable.

He flings her hand away.

Comes the irresolution that accompanies all surety.

Struggle to break free, she thinks. Lean in, she thinks. You who have neglected so much. Rose, always so difficult, so troubled, impossible. Many things to be cut down so love can rise up out of the ruins.

She is giving Henry the short end of the stick. Of course the sex is wonderful. Of course it is.

The hips are one place in the body where old pain is stored. Breathe into the hips. With each exhalation imagine a line of silver light ascending from the hips toward the top of your skull, with each inhalation imagine a line of silver light plunging through the crown of your head and along your spine down into your hips. Can you feel a slight opening? Can you surrender a little more into the pose? Try not to close around ideas now forming in your mind. Try to let the tension pour out with the breath.

EIGHT

YOU ARE SEVENTY-TWO years old when it occurs to you to ask
Jill, the Picton Gallery owner, if she would curate an exhibition
of your watercolours. She arrives at the lake to browse three
decades' worth, created in shades of creamy egg yolk, pale salmon,
soft violet. Abstracts, mostly, horizontal lines, layer upon milky
layer of pale colour. A few portraits. Lakes and skies, immense
and sympathetic, each to each, the curator says, though this is
not quite right, she can see she's off the mark. Your pictures are
of a different order, an alignment of spaciousness and uncanny
light. What is the force of the form? Jill asks. It's a paradox, that
force — strangely peaceful, it blows the mind apart.

You agree to a September show. You will frame thirty of the
selected works, and Jill will do the rest. She doesn't know what

your watercolours might be worth, but the prices she suggests are absurd; the art world has gone mad. About this you say nothing.

Using a double-sided adhesive, she attaches to the gallery wall small cards bearing titles and prices. Eight hundred dollars. One thousand dollars. She says the public is going to go gaga. How you wish Teresa were alive to see the Picton public go gaga over your strange paintings.

Henry is drunk, has been drinking since three in the afternoon after successfully donating the last of his father's things to the local thrift shop, which leaves him free to flee the county, the province, the whole fucking country. This happy fact necessitates a trip to the fields behind the house with two bottles of red wine. He drinks, resolutely, then lies sprawled on his back in the grass.

With his pen raised he attempts to catch the movement of his thoughts. These are like sludge below clouds, a momentary slurry of shit he soon discovers cannot be expressed, not with lines. Furious, he throws the pen away, hard.

In his agitation he runs from the fields all the way into town. Already drunk, he goes to the bar where dealers go, and there he is the animal it would pain him to display in front of Ydessa. But Ydessa is nowhere, she's glad to be rid of him.

In a cupboard in the basement of his father's house he had found a box labelled *Henry's Observations*. In it were his notebooks and sketchbooks from childhood and early years in Picton. It came as a surprise and a relief to realize his father had liked his airy sketches of the world enough to keep them. His father's long silences. Henry had tried not to break these. Silence was his father's chapel, erected to keep out the unholy. Silence would not be the choice for him, son of a long line of men who spent their lives falling, failing. Were his drawings akin to words? Knowing his own reticence, his own perversity, very, very unlikely. He'd joined the line, hadn't he. Fucking losers, all.

Do you think you have to renounce everything? he had yelled at Ydessa. Is that it? Even renounce loyalty?

She had looked into her hands and said nothing.

You know what I think? I think you're still a drinking adult, but now you drink a poison you call virtue. You've scrimped to buy just one grand picture of a way of life, and you're drunk on it.

A great black shadow having been hurled, he had flinched but kept on. There isn't anything you'll stop for. No one you'll stop for, just you and the cosmos, is that it? Is that freedom? I don't see how it's freedom if you won't accept the authority of your own desire.

She had turned her head away. You want to be careful, Henry. Here I am, loving you. The power goes down, you think I have released you from some old struggle, flung you in a new direction.

At least I remember where sweetness lies. At least I remember where honey is.

Where is your honey? Can you point to it? No. Nothing is fixed. Don't go falling in love with your anticipated outcomes, Henry, or they will wreck you. Dead bees by the millions, and clearly do we see that no honey is everlasting. Let us love a little while we can.

He leaves the bar thoroughly unhinged. In the flickering light falling from shop and café windows, he watches his feet as they shuffle, as if disembodied, along the sidewalk, absorbed by their sluggish rhythm. He thinks he will draw the faltering pace, then remembers that he flung his pen away. He looks up, sees a sandwich board. *Opening tonight. Watercolours by Barri Grew.* The muscles in his upper arms contract.

He is too drunk to see Barri, the one who took him in, who went looking for him when he was in danger of the deepest sort of neglect. Barri. Was he a basket case until she rescued him? And what did she do when she found him? Just take him in. Accept him. Find him interesting. Make it possible for him to go to Baptiste Lake almost every weekend, to paint and draw with her.

Your father won't mind? she had asked.

Gone to fields. He won't care.

You had arrived at the Picton high school at noon. Sitting in your old truck, you watched the kids jerk down the front steps, not a thought in their heads. And there, loitering to one side was the easily recognizable fourteen-year-old Henry, angular, tall, shaggy, his long hair falling over his eyes. Collapsed in the rib cage, looking down at his feet. But beautiful. You got out of the truck and stood, holding your jean jacket close, watching him as he came toward you. He was a maelstrom of thinking, this much was obvious, his eyes unfocused, his body ill-registered.

Henry?

Your voice was low and stern.

Henry Rattle.

He slowed.

You remember me, Henry?

He looked up.

Oh.

You extended your hand and Henry looked at it as if it were a thing on fire, to shake it an impossibility.

Can I give you a lift?

Huh?

You were already tiring of his performance, saying, I have come to, what? Get you back, regain an old friendship. I would like to know you. I hope you might like to know me.

You stopped, said no more.

Did Teresa die? He nudged a stone with the toe of his shoe.

Surprised, you could only say Yes. The year you moved away, in the spring.

Did Ydessa remarry?

I know nothing about Ydessa.

And so it was you started up again, without Teresa, without Ydessa. On weekends you drove down to Picton to collect him from his father's house, and the two of you spent happy hours together with the cat named Blue. His father's disapproval of you was short-lived.

Don't know why you want to hang around with that old dyke.

The terrible conversations only with himself ended. This was why.

How many portraits of Henry did you make, huddled together on the dock, steamer blankets draped heavily over your laps? Through the changing seasons of five full years, rascal blue jays calling in the jack pine overhead, his pen raised, your brush upheld, diligent in your slow vision, you brought together the harmonies that energy brings to energy. Dropping down deeply into focused work, the mind settling, drinking coffee and, at day's end, wine, the years flowed. Autumn he loved. For him you were autumn. Flannel shirts and the wood stove and a fiery interest in all he thought and did, with no letup to the sorrow you felt for the absence of Teresa.

A day never went by, he knew, that you did not think of her. He came to know Teresa through the intelligence of your sorrow.

Pushing through Henry's arguments, his father's disinterest, you successfully sent him to university, and the days in his company came to an end.

Now he is drunk at the door of Barri's opening, and he must go in. He will be an embarrassment, but he must go in. A nausea takes hold of him, he stumbles around the corner of the building and is sick, a sudden and not unkind release. He wipes his mouth with the back of his hand, tucks his shirt properly into his jeans, and rounds the building to the gallery door.

You observe the density of colour that clings to Henry as he stands at the door, transfixed. A little knot of tension forms at the back of your throat. You have not seen him in two years, though you know of his father's suicide. A terrible sin, Jill had said, emphasizing what Henry had had to do alone, with the body. Now here he is, an uproar on two legs. To enter into this will surely be a mistake, but you go to him where he is weeping and coughing and sputtering, gasping as he cries out to you. What a faltering wreckage of a young man. You crush him to your breast.

BORROW A POOL where trees can weep
    Borrow the tree at the heart of the world
    Borrow a sword beneath water lily
    Borrow heat to marry bone
    Borrow hunger, borrow cold
    Borrow cornflower in blue bloom
    Borrow the attribute of drowning
    Borrow strange feet that can hold.

If you hear music coming from the apartment next door, or voices passing in the street, notice them, allow them, but then allow them to dissolve. This is will pass. Step your right foot forward into a lunge, and hold.

She snaps her fingers softly to a count of five.

Step your left foot forward and hold in Padahastasana. Two. Three. Four. Five. Now lift, arms out to the side, and hold. Now back again. Padahastasana. *Surya Namaskar.*

The students are wiry with effort. She breathes the whole room into a sensation each feels, and lets it go. All is pulsating, all is fluctuating. A siren sounds in the distance, roaring toward them, through the windows, and is gone, leaving its afterimage of confusion, of emergency, which labours along the floorboards before draining away. She asks them to notice. Notice, now draw your attention back to your breath.

In Savasana, a student begins to sob, her throttled cries like a small animal sputtering at the back of the room. Some of the other students begin to shift, their discomfort ill-contained. She sits in the lotus position and watches the pressure of emotion flood the air.

Seven minutes pass; she rings the Tibetan bell, softly at first, then louder, twice more. Bring your attention back to the breath, she says, her voice fierce as well as tender. The room is an orgy of relief.

As the bolsters and eye pillows and blankets are packed away, an older student approaches her with a question it's clear she is loath to ask. She makes some small talk then says breathlessly, I wonder if you could tell me what enlightenment is?

Ydessa laughs lightly. No, I don't think I could.

The woman, though unsteadily, persists.

My daughter says that by becoming aware of my breathing I take a step closer to enlightenment. She says that if I concentrate on my breathing I will interrupt unconscious thinking and thereby be closer to enlightenment. I wonder if yoga is some kind of religious experience, and whether it is acceptable to the Church.

Ah, the Church. She smiles again. I don't know. Breathing happens without our willing it, a small and, if you will permit me, a sacred activity. To notice it might be revolutionary. There's a vast intelligence in it. Let me ask you: did your daughter send you to yoga?

The woman nods. My daughter thinks I am losing it.

Losing it?

Changing, but in the wrong way.

It has been her practice, on hearing pronouncements such as these, to wait. Wait for what comes next, for what is surely coming. In circumstances such as these, she is prepared to wait eight minutes, the exact length of time it takes for the sun's light to reach earth. She makes the calculation. The silence can undo some people, often does. The woman catches her breath.

I have been dating —. She pauses, faltering. I've been having sex with a much younger man.

Henry's image lifts and falls within the weak smile she manages to offer this student whose hands are wringing an eye pillow like a wet cloth. You are wondering if yoga will help you conduct your life in ways acceptable to God.

The woman looks to her feet, overcome. Put this way, my question seems absurd. No. But perhaps you are right. Am I looking for something to run to for approval?

Shame is without end.

I'll try another class with you. I won't say no quite yet.

Seated at the wooden desk where she conducts the business of Spirit Level, she overhears one student say to another, She must be raking it in. The bathroom is state-of-the-art: go look at the awesome Tetris sink. Amazing.

And it strikes her then: she must find Henry. Only she distrusts this desire with all her being, mistrusting the lust that gathers in her centre. Seek him how? Tumescent and striving? But. She is *required* to find him: she sees this. To seek him is what arrives, therefore go willingly. This has been her practice: do what is in front of you to do.

Glorious release from compulsion.

Whitney will have googled Henry and his bees. Is it too late to catch the boy she once said she would put down her life for? She will not sacrifice the studio — her life — not even for Henry, and even though she can't bear the pigheadedness she feels, thinking this, she has long understood the fleeting nature of chance, and here is a chance, surely, to move in his direction. She feels she is forgetting some words she once believed in. Go or stay? Leave him alone or go after him? Intervene or observe?

Nothing is required of her. Isn't this true? Free to hold both the form of Henry's unhappiness and the form of her own constriction? Free to love and be loved? It occurs to her that she is failing as never before. She bends her heart toward that long-ago Baptiste window where Henry lifted his arm to point the way to Millionaire's Island. Just follow the sun path.

The sapphire glints on her upturned palm.

She is still a drinking adult.

Barri places a cup of hot black coffee on the table in front of Henry. Drink this. She sits in the chair opposite, quiet, unobtrusive. Studies him. He allows this, glad of her attention. She can leave him alone or she can ask questions, it's all the same to him. Is there anything in the world he would refuse her? No.

The wind is dropping, across the lake an arrival repeats itself in wave after wave of foaming grey. The leaves make a grab for the night, to shake it. When the headlights had flashed, briefly, exploding on the thick trees along the drive, he thought he saw their red complexion, their leaves turning though it is only September. Tomorrow he'll see what colour there is.

To be in Barri's house is an astonishing comfort. His body hangs on his bones. He drinks the coffee. He makes homelessness the theme of his thoughts. In a recurring dream he had stood behind his father, watching over his shoulder as he gathered his bees into a kind of small ball, holding them in his bare hands, wrapping their tiny bodies, startlingly yellow, in golden honey. Uproarious patterns are threatening to paralyze the emotion he carries, the comfort of being with Barri. Where will he go? he wonders. Out west. Be able assistant to some reputable California beekeeper, anonymous assistant, strange and disciplined. So much for a fine arts degree. The only thing he knows is bees and honey. There is nothing for him here.

The sad and tender heart not scoffed at, never bullied, never mimicked; it enters the public school classroom at nine years of age and discovers bullies, discovers mimics, learns how bullies are woven into the very fabric of every endeavour. At Baptiste his heart had sought the deepest patterns, inaccessible to those who look with their eyes only. Meeting irony and other twisted surface embellishments, he began his long apprenticeship in forgetting.

Lying next to her in her bed, Henry had shared stories with Ydessa. She told him about the ashram, where, she said, she began to learn what he had understood in childhood. Beauty first. How pathetic that she had left human society at the very moment when, forced by circumstance, he had gained a world thick with greed, vengefulness, and envy, with denial and accusation, craving and aversion, the whole arsenal of human armour and weaponry, the whole theatre of human suffering, which adolescence reveals.

It's a glorious September afternoon at Baptiste, summer residents packed up and gone, the air quiet save for a light wind, which ruffles leaves in the treetops. It moves like muscle, like water.

He watches you painting happily at the far end of the dock, your easel placed at an angle that allows you to observe both him and the lake. You mark the canvas. He can see a milky salmon begin to form.

Before you moved off to fetch your watercolours, you two had been discussing what he should do with the box of sketchbooks found in his father's basement. And now it's decided: you'll keep them for him if he'll allow you to look through them any time the mood strikes. How close he had come to burning them.

You withdraw easily from conversation, hailed by an old and rigorous discipline. You carry little ambivalence about withdrawal from him, who, it must be said, is not steady without you as his prop. Standing at your easel, you move into your own private act of devotion. The boundaries between you and Henry are clear, and, being so clear, he can see that his side is devoid of any kind of discipline.

Once there was his ardent commitment to drawing. Once he took up his pen with the deepest sort of curiosity. Once his days were consumed with thinking about the beautiful, everlasting flux that alters with the conditions of the world, contemplating the meaning of his mother's adage.

He had told you about calling on Ydessa, about his months in Toronto, about being with Ydessa on the night of the blackout. As he spoke, tightness grabbed at his throat. You could see the hot tears forming. You watched him with the greatest of sympathy but did not reach for him. You watched his words falter.

You told him your idea. There were no children, no nieces or nephews you wished to entrust the property to, but, you said, were he interested, you would leave it all to him in a heartbeat. Begin a new life here, take up the arts, where he belongs. Why not?

You'll live a long time, he protested. I have to find my own way.

You did the math for him. Come back to Baptiste to bury me. Then stay.

Now, watching as Barri pauses to observe the lake, seeing her move her brush over the surface of her canvas, he achieves a feeling akin to breath, as if observing Barri and the lake were inhale, exhale, all breath, all living, everything a part of one fluid chance. She bows to the canvas and allows her hand to make a leaping, nervous salmon — coloured lines. They no sooner wet the paper than a form appears. Watching, he sees that he must seize his own hour.

He removes from his back pocket the fountain pen Barri bought him, opens a new sketchbook, and begins, observing her, moving the pen in nervous inky lines over the surface of his paper. What could be more nerve-racking, more terrifying and satisfying than this lonesome effort? Together once more, called by some indomitable force away from the noise of the world, with leaves shuffling overhead and heavy voices murmuring over the water. Their recent conversation, the agreement and plan, then the lapse into long silence, has called up a strange, demanding, otherworldly reality. It suddenly, forcibly, demands his attention. Why? Why let this force rule? Does he take up his pen involuntarily or decisively, roused to trace the rhythm that is Barri at her end of the dock, beloved friend, slow at her easel?

There is a between-point, a still point, in which all desires cease, all capacity is thwarted, a gap that is the death of will and doubt alike. He looks at the first line he has made. Terrible, the opposite of artful. *Give it up*, a voice whispers.

The drawing will be added to the boxful of others and placed in some closet to close out the years. Why allow that?

Then, in a breath, released out of the hollow is a slow, heavy hand that not so much moves as is moved, released, flickering and dancing. His hand is a stenographer, recording what it receives, parabolas and curves of living, borne along currents of air on music not heard but felt, an exchange with life, his life, his mind creating out of its depths scenes, words, images, an expression of unnameable pain — Ydessa upturned in a handstand, *Love, please be true*, the awful suffering needed to prove the world.

Hello, Barri. It's Ydessa Bloom.
Ydessa. Well now. I think I can guess why you're calling.
Silence.
He's not here.

He isn't.

No.

But he was there?

Yes.

How long?

A few weeks.

Did he say anything? About where he would go, I mean?

He's gone to California.

California? But why?

He's sold his father's things, he's sold most of his own things.

Did he talk to you about me?

A little.

Did he ask for your advice?

No, he never did.

Can you tell me how to reach him?

She tells Ydessa what she knows, holding the receiver tightly, pulling the mouthpiece close so there's no mistaking what she says next.

Leave him alone, Ydessa. He'll be fine without you.

In New York Keith had told her, People want me to stop giving away my art for free. When Roger and I found out that Jonathan had AIDS, we went to the East River and cried and cried. After crying's done, you figure out how you're going to deal with loss, how you're going to face it. There aren't too many choices.

She waited for him to carry on.

Art is very healing, though this has not been explored scientifically. I like the idea of arty things lasting longer than humans can, existing in places where people can see them for a long time. Most people aren't very skilled at opening up fully at the crossroads where things happen. Art is good at that.

Weather, the forces of the unconscious, its tremendous fluctuations, seen through and beyond you and me: in this age of utter self-involvement, utter narcissism, I want to find a way to live in the city without unreliable props. Possessions, drama, power — unnatural air, unnatural light. I try to live alone, conscious of my daily bread, alone in community, alone in inner and outer weather.

A failure, is what you think. Still a drinking person, you say. But Henry, I am not isolating myself so much as trying to forge my own path. To commit the sin of living as I see fit, where once I was stymied. Perhaps it's my independence that annoys you.

She shifts closer.

Sometimes, throughout many years of yoga practice, to work meant to sit, eyes closed, listening to the hubbub of mind and ego, my ego eager to do and to be praised for doing. But now I'm listening for something else. Let's say I am listening for the voice of each particular moment.

He laughs.

Laugh if you must. Go ahead. But I do believe that to celebrate singularity, to celebrate the particular, is to live in direct opposition to centuries of unworkable, dehumanizing forces.

He feels her as a backlash in himself, catching mean spirit full force in a place at the very bottom of his heart.

———

I can't explain it to you, Henry. It can't be explained, only experienced. I love you and I love everything that has happened to bring us together. I love the past and the future equally. To be alive, even within the hours of painful uncertainty, is to me a joy, an unrelenting joy.

Then you must have seen something good happening when the power went out? Why else did you take off your clothes?

He will lose the thread of their connection, this she knows as much as she knows anything. Nothing she can say to him will sound true.

There are moments in my living when living quickens. Intensity quickens. Times to celebrate. I have set an intention to remain single; I haven't initiated lovemaking in years.

You make it sound like such a whimsical decision.

Whimsy. Yes, she says after a while, I suppose it could look like that. A caprice, you're thinking, or maybe a prank, when a woman fails to fear the aftermath of a sexual act. Fickle, you're thinking: a woman who behaves this way. But I can't reduce what has happened between us to an equation, which logic would have me do.

So it was simply seize the day.

No, it wasn't *simply* anything. What I'm saying is more complex than you allow. It was all we shared at Baptiste: your mother's ring, Roger's arm, the losses that have accumulated for each of us over the years, the many adjustments we've made. It was a whole line of experience. It was our whole lives. My living is in no way different than that of hundreds of thousands of other people's, but when such a living quickens, even for only a few hours, it's hosanna.

Imagination comes in waves, from ancient times, across the years. Every symbol is liquid at its root. Try to let all pictures flow. Our lovemaking is glorious, a modern picture.

Here's a good one, this one more ancient. A recipe: How to get Bees from an Ox. Take a two-year-old ox into a small house with four windows and an empty hearth. Stopper its nose and mouth with blue cloth. Bludgeon it to death. Lay cassia, thyme, and branches on the body. Wait.

But nothing is established. The habits and systems I keep are for breaking. I'm not addicted to my methods, you know.

You can stop with the speech, Ydessa. I'm not your student. It's fine. I like it here. The California sun suits me. Assistant bee-keeper suits me.

The poet says not every labour will come to sweetness in the end.

It'll have to be all right. You aren't inviting me to fly back to Toronto with you. Weren't you only ever doing yourself a favour? Haven't I always been your wrong end? At Baptiste, and in Toronto, at the worst possible moments in my life, I tried to give myself to you. I wanted to make something between us that would last.

INSTRUCTOR

But this is not necessarily where we end. Can you envision a present that holds no promises? Bear to look at me, Henry. To see the love that is here. Come away from that window.

He turns, seeking first a place for himself alone, now, and in the bright unbearable months ahead, one that will always welcome him. He picks up his pen, his sketchbook.

His solar plexus opens, a threshold.

Her living mind goes forth, like a spider, like a needle, threading his wild heart. His bones are magical; like night the sex is dark. Sting me, Bee.

He groans as she cries out, they both drop away from the other without an answer back, they descend, carrying tight against their chests words to secrete through the underworld.

This is the suspension of grief: nothing remains to crane toward, the future is too subtle. Nothing remains beyond a foreground faith, senses quickening against a picture only she can see, of strange, exquisite, fleeting economies.

I used my own heartbreak to decorate myself, she tells him, naked in his arms.

Yes, he laughs, reducing your life to eleven shades of white.

Train your thoughts to return to your head, there to make honey. When shelter is rare, bees will nest in skulls and other bones. Be a shelter for ten thousand and one unfixed ideas: bees will dance there.

In growing heat from the rising sun, under the brightening leaves, in bee buzz rap, in prayer that comes unbidden: the lonely They who would be known. She hears footsteps. It's Henry, come to tell her that the taxi has arrived.

| END |

N O T E S

I was aided in the writing of the work by many texts, poems, phrases, and books. In particular: *Yoga*, by Mircea Eliade; *Pilgrim at Tinker Creek*, by Annie Dillard; Walt Whitman's "Song of Myself"; "The Spider," by Loren Eiseley; *Stars: A Fully Illustrated, Authoritative, and Easy-to-Use Guide*, by Robert H. Baker and Herbert S. Zim (Golden Guide, St. Martin's Press, 2001); *Song of Roland*; Virginia Woolf, *The Waves*; *The Yoga Sutras*, by Swami Satchidananda; *The Maiden Tsar*, by Robert Bly and Marion Woodman; *The Creation of Consciousness*, by Edward F. Edinger; *Yoga and the Quest for the True Self*, by Stephen Cope; the poems of Dionne Brand, Louise Glück, Adrienne Rich, Karen Solie; other novels by Virginia Woolf.

ACKNOWLEDGEMENTS

My deepest gratitude to the following people, each of whom helped to keep the vision of the novel alive over fourteen years: Felicia and Ante Pavlovic, Stan Dragland, Jennifer Glossop, James Langer, Alana Wilcox, Yeats McNally, Robin Penney, Cheryl Fenk, Danielle Flynn, Helena Butler, Melanie Caines, mentors at Banff Writing Studio 2015 — Tessa McWatt, John Burnside — and fellow Studio participants.

Thanks to the hundreds of volunteers who keep the traditions of Vipassana meditation going strong at courses in Vipassana centres around the world.

Thanks to artist Anita Singh for permission to use her artwork on the cover of *Instructor*.

An ArtsNL grant allowed me to secure time away from Pedlar Press activities to focus on the novel. I am indebted to ArtsNL and other councils across Canada for their indomitable labours in support of artists and art production.

My humble thanks to everyone at Breakwater Books: Rebecca Rose, Rhonda Molloy, Jocelyne Thomas, Samantha Fitzpatrick, and Marianne Ward.

Stan Dragland has given me hundreds of precious days in which to converse about reading and writing in Canada, and for these conversations I am entirely blessed.

Beth Follett is the founder and publisher of Pedlar Press, a Canadian literary house. Her first novel, *Tell It Slant* (Coach House Books, 2001), a retelling of Djuna Barnes's 1936 novel *Nightwood*, met with critical acclaim. Her poetry, prose, and nonfiction work have appeared in *Brick*, *Best Canadian Poetry 2019*, and elsewhere. She lives in St. John's, NL.